THE WHITE DEER

Other books by
JAMES THURBER

MY WORLD— AND WELCOME TO IT
MEN, WOMEN AND DOGS
THE BEAST IN ME AND OTHER ANIMALS

For children
MANY MOONS
THE GREAT QUILLOW

THE
WHITE
DEER

JAMES THURBER

Drawings by the author

A HARVEST BOOK
HARCOURT BRACE & COMPANY
San Diego   New York   London

To
Joe and Gertrude and Nora

CONTENTS

THE WHITE DEER

THE MAGICAL FOREST

If you should walk and wind and wander far enough on one of those afternoons in April when smoke goes down instead of up, and nearby things sound far away and far things near, you are more than likely to come at last to the enchanted forest that lies between the Moonstone Mines and Centaurs Mountain. You'll know the woods when you are still a long way off by vir-tue of a fragrance you can never quite forget and never quite remember. And there'll be a distant bell that causes boys to run and laugh and girls to stand and tremble. If you pluck one of the ten thousand toadstools that grow in the emerald grass at the edge of the wonderful woods, it will feel as heavy as a hammer in your hand, but if you let it go it will sail away over the trees like a tiny parachute, trailing black and purple stars.

There's even a tale, first told by minstrels in the medieval time, that rabbits here can tip their heads as men now tip their hats, removing them with their paws and putting them back again.

This enchanted forest was once upon a time a part of the kingdom of a mighty monarch named Clode, who had three sons, Thag, Gallow and Jorn. Thag and Gallow, like their father, King Clode, were great hunters, and when they were not eating or sleeping they were engaged in the chase. Jorn, the youngest and shortest of the Princes—he was only six feet tall—was a poet and musician, and when he was not at table or in bed, he was fond of setting his verses to the music of the lyre. He occasionally took part in the hunt when his father and brothers insisted, but he was careful to

loose his arrows
and cast his lances
clear of whatever
quarry the royal
family might be
pursuing.

Three times in
the middle of the
century in which they lived, the King and his two older
sons had depleted their kingdom of wild life, and three
times they had been forced to wait around the castle, restlessly stringing their bows, feathering their arrows and
sharpening their lances, until a new generation of deer and
wild boar could come to maturity in the fields and forests.
King Clode and Thag and Gallow ate oftener, drank more,
and slept longer during these tedious periods of inactivity,
and they fell to buffeting and plaguing the members of their
retinue, particularly a dwarf named Quondo, and the Royal
Wizard, a castle wizard whose magic consisted chiefly of
sleight-of-hand and juggling, since he was not privy to
the secrets of the woods wizards who lived in the enchanted
forest.

Jorn found these seasons serene, and spent his time singing of a faraway Princess who would one day set a perilous
labor for each of the Princes to perform. He sang that love,
not might, would untie the magic knot, or open the mystic

5

lock, or hoodwink the dreadful dragon or resolve whatever other problem the faraway Princess might propose as the key to her heart and hand. Thag and Gallow guffawed at their younger brother's "finickery" as they called it, and they would take to tossing Quondo, the dwarf, back and forth in the air as if he were a ball, oblivious of his guttural protests. The older brothers knew better than to put upon Jorn for he had more than once taken falls from them in wrestling, and he could hold his own at tilting on horse-back.

One night when the third period of waiting for the boar and the deer to venture abroad still had a hundred moons to run, King Clode told a tale to his sons, over his tankards, while Jorn strummed softly on his lyre and Quondo sat in a dark corner of the banquet hall, under a great shield, nursing his scars and bruises.

"There is always the enchanted forest to hunt," Prince Thag had growled at supper time, testing the string of a long bow.

"There is always the enchanted forest to shun," King Clode had roared, and he went on to tell of how he had once dared to chase a fleet deer in the magic woods with his own father and two brothers, and how they had brought the deer to bay against the sheer wall of Centaurs Mountain, and how as they made ready to launch their arrows, the deer had been transformed into a tall, dark young prin-

6

cess, who had been changed into a deer years before by a wicked old woman jealous of the young girl's beauty.

"There we were," went on King Clode, "your grand-father, King Bode, and his three sons—your Uncle Cloon, your Uncle Garf and myself—feeling like sheep in our cha-grin and dismay, or like a mastiff that goes growling boldly into a wolf's den and comes upon a pink-eyed female rabbit. One of those grinning woods wizards came along presently and conjured up a white palfrey for the Princess—out of thin air, as I remember it—and we rode off to the castle.

"We gave the Princess food and wine and a pillow for her head, and on the following day we set off in full pano-ply and jingling trappings to carry her to her father, a king whose lands lay far to the north. We jin-gled through apple blos-soms, as we started out,  for it was May, and we jingled through snowflakes when we neared her ancestral castle. Her father and mother were overjoyed to see their daughter again and her father the King set a series of passable tables in honor of the occasion, although to my taste the wines of the North smack a bit of buckle polish, or lance oil, it may be—this was many years ago."

"Why have you never told—" said Thag.

"—this tale before?" said Gallow.

"You were too young," said Clode, "for such a tale as might offend the growing heart. . . . Where was I?"

"This was many years ago," Thag prompted.

"Ah, yes," said Clode. "Well, your grandfather and your uncles and I were eager to set off for home and the chase. The Princess' father was a fellow of small fancies, with an indoor turn of mind, given to dawdling over the chess board even in the keenest hunting weather, drinking a warmish wassail full of aloes or something.

"We were not to get off as soon or as easy as we thought. There was the infernal custom of the country whereby a rescued princess exercises the privilege of claiming one of her rescuers as her husband. She was a pretty enough gray-

eyed minx but she was fond of the harp and the spinnet, with no stomach for the chase, and a way of fluttering up behind a man before he knew it, moving like a cat on velvet.

"The upshot was that your grandfather rode home alone and the Princess set Cloon and Garf and myself each a perilous labor. Cloon was to bring back the golden right wing of the great Falcon of Ferralane. Garf, an uncouth varlet at best, though an angel in the saddle, was sent to bring back a drop of blood from the right index finger of a hundred kings, an adventure which could not conceivably be concluded within the life span of the human being; and I was told off to fetch the Princess an enormous diamond said to lie between the paws of a fearful creature, half dragon and half roc, in the cave of a mountain not many leagues distant."

King Clode filled up two tankards from a bowl of wine on the table before him and drank them off.

"You were too young to remember," he continued, "but a traveler from faraway Ferralane passed this way some twenty years ago with the news that your Uncle Cloon was bested in his struggle with the great Falcon whose *left* wing, it transpired during the battle, was made of edged and pointed steel. Your Uncle Garf has never been heard from to this day, which is reasonable enough in view of estimates arrived at by my Royal Recorder, who has figured that it requires ninety-seven years to procure a drop of blood from the right index finger of a hundred kings."

While the King filled his tankards again with wine, Prince Jorn strummed a sorrowful song on his lyre.

"To make a rather distressing story short," resumed King Clode, "the monster I was dispatched to overcome proved to be made of clay and boxwood, so that it was the simplest of tasks to deprive the creature of the enormous diamond clutched between its artificial paws. I delivered the stone to the Princess and won her hand in marriage, having already won the fair lady's heart, as even Quondo there can see."

The King sat back in his great chair and closed his eyes.

"And the moral of this tale," grumbled Quondo, "is precisely what?"

The King opened one eye. "The moral of this tale," he said, "is precisely never hunt deer in the enchanted forest."

Thag and Gallow, who had sat staring at their father through his recital, looked at each other and at the King again.

"We do not like it," said Thag.

"Our mother having once been a deer!" said Gallow.

Jorn spoke for the first time. "It was but the illusory and meaningless shape of magic," he said, and returned to his music.

"The boy has it," roared King Clode. "It was as he says —meaningless magic." He tapped a tankard on the table top. "Never quite got used to it, though," he admitted at last. "Don't suppose a hunting man ever could." There was a long and thoughtful silence before Clode spoke again. "She took to her chamber of a mortal malady shortly after Jorn was born, and never set foot on the stair again."

"Perhaps she died of a fall," said Thag.

"Perhaps she died of a surfeit," said Gallow.

"Perhaps she died of a look," said Jorn.

The King hurled a tankard at the youngest Prince and

Jorn caught it in mid-air.

"Has his mother's quickness and his mother's grace," muttered Clode. He sighed. "Well, there is the tale."

The Royal High Chamberlain's voice spoke suddenly behind Clode's chair, and the King started slightly. "Must I have men who creep about like cats?" roared Clode.

"There is a minstrel, Sire," the Royal High Chamberlain said.

"Then send him in, then send him in!" cried Clode. "He'll sing to us of strong men and the chase. I've had enough of sorrow and of love." He glared at Jorn.

The minstrel entered softly and sat upon a stool and strummed his lute and sang. He sang of a white deer, a white deer with the speed of light, a white deer as lovely to look upon as a waterfall in springtime.

When the song was done, the King asked, "Is this deer as swift as light and as lovely as a waterfall in springtime a creature of your silly fancy, or does it have breath and blood that I and my sons may test its speed and strength?"

The minstrel sang:

> "The white deer flashes like the light
> Through the forest day and night."

"Name me the name of this forest," roared the King. The minstrel sang:

The White Deer

"By night and day the white deer shines
Betwixt the Mountain and the Mines."

At this King Clode rose from his chair, upsetting a tankard of red wine that spilled onto the floor. "You bound the enchanted forest with your infernal rhyme!" he cried. "No man of King Clode's household hunts in those accursed woods!"

The minstrel sang:

"Too swift for Thag, too quick for Gallow,
Too strong for young Prince Jorn to follow,
But foot of turtle, heart of toad
Never shall be spoke of Clode."

The King pulled at his long black mustaches and a light flickered in his eye and went out and flickered again like the light of a firefly. "Mayhap," he said at last, "this white deer with the speed of light is a true deer. We shall test its vaunted prowess on the morrow. If it be a true deer, I shall hang its head upon the wall and its meat in the larder. If it be a lovely maiden enchanted by some witch's or wizard's spell, the daughter of some king whose lands lie to the north or east or south or west, I shall drive my lance and arrow through this foolish minstrel's heart!"

King Clode pounded a tankard on the table to accent each word of his ominous warning, but when he looked around, the minstrel had disappeared. King Clode frowned.

"Fellow bore a remarkable resemblance to somebody or other I have encountered somewhere or other," he muttered.

"If this be a true deer," said Thag, "we shall enjoy the greatest chase in history."

"If this be a true deer," said Gallow, "we shall hang the finest venison in all the world."

The King's eyes gleamed as he swallowed a great apricot.

"And if this be a true Princess of the royal blood?" It was the rumbling voice of Quondo, the dwarf, speaking from his corner. The King hurled an apple at the dwarf, but Jorn caught it in the air.

"If this be a true Princess of the royal blood," Jorn said, "she shall set the sons of Clode each a perilous labor to find the Prince most worthy of her heart and hand."

At this, to show their strength, Thag caught up a heavy iron from the fireplace and bent it double, and Gallow turned a double handspring down the floor. Jorn watched his brothers and stroked the strings of his lyre. The King tugged at his mustaches, his eyes burning with dreams of the chase. Quondo sat in his corner under the shield, watching Clode and Thag and Gallow, and listening to the music of Jorn's lyre.

The next morning as the sun was rising, the King and his three sons, riding on black chargers, entered the enchanted forest, reined in and gazed about them.

"Pick not that buttercup," said Clode, pointing a leathery finger at a small flower in the emerald grass, "or it will turn to flame and burn your hand."

"Do not pluck the lichen from that tree," said Thag, "or it will turn to blood and stain your hand."

"Do not touch that white stone there," said Gallow, "or

it will come alive and bite your hand."

There was thunder suddenly from behind the Moonstone Mines, the sun went out, a flash of lightning made the four horses tremble and in the darkness all around the King and his sons glimmered a million fireflies.

While Clode and his sons gazed at the shimmering dance in amazement, the fireflies changed to snowflakes which fell softly to the earth and disappeared. The thunder ceased, the clouds parted and the sun came out again.

"These constant tricks upon the eye are bad for man's digestion," said King Clode. "I shall have no stomach for the finest meat on earth if this false flux of fact and form does not desist."

"What's hot is cold," said Thag.

"What's hard is soft," said Gallow.

"What's night is day," said Clode.

Jorn, who had been thinking up a verse during the show of marvels, recited it:

> *"What's black is white,*
> *What's red is blue,*
> *What's dark is light,*
> *What's true is true."*

"Well rhymed, Prince Jorn," said a voice that seemed to come from nowhere until the King and his sons looked down and saw a woods wizard in a blue robe and a red peaked cap.

"Ho," said the King, glaring at the wizard, "have I not seen you otherwhere than here?"

"You have seen me otherwhen than now," said the sorcerer, plucking a pansy and tossing it into the air where it became a butterfly and fluttered away through the trees.

"I have ridden in these woods but once before," said King Clode.

"Twenty-six years, twenty-five days and twenty-four hours ago," said the wizard.

"My father and my brothers and I pursued a deer," said Clode, "which against the wall of Centaurs Mountain underwent a marvelous and mortifying metamorphosis. I am a little touchy on the topic, too, so do not turn your tongue to taunts."

"He does not turn *his* tongue," said Jorn. "He twists your own, to 'm's' and 't's.' "

"And 'w's,' " said the wizard, "as you shall see."

"Try twice that trick on Tlode," said the King, with great dignity, "my mousey man of magic, and we will wid these wids of woozards." King Clode made a royal gesture of arrogance, authority and austerity, while his sons stared at him in astonishment.

"You speak magic words, O Clode," said the wizard, smugly, removing his cap and bowing deeply. "And now may I be of service to you and the Princes Thag and Gallow and Jorn? May I show you the barking tree, or the musical mud, or the wingless birds?"

The King grimaced at this list of wonders and Prince Jorn answered the wizard. "My father seeks the white deer," he said, "the white deer swift as light and lovely as a waterfall in springtime."

The wizard bowed again and flung his cap in the air. "What goes up must not come down," he said, and the cap, swinging slowly like a bell, sailed silently over the trees, rising higher and higher until finally it could be seen no more.

"What comes down must go up," said the wizard, and he wiggled three fingers of his left hand toward the ground. Suddenly the snowflakes that had melted and vanished began to rise from the earth and when they were as high as the wizard's heart, they changed into a million fireflies. The King and his sons watched in wonder and for a moment four horses and four men were as still as statues in amazement, for through the glow and glimmer and gleam there suddenly flashed a white deer as swift as light and as lovely as a waterfall in springtime.

"Hoy, yollo!" cried the King, and he and his sons were

off in pursuit, the sparks from their horses' hoofs joining in the dance of the fireflies.

The white deer flashed through the green forest and the King and his sons followed, past the barking tree, across the musical mud, in and out of a flock of wingless birds. On and on went the chase until the sun began to set and long strange shadows fell. The white deer led its pursuers through a silver swamp and a bronze bog and a golden glade, its speed still swift as light. It shot like an arrow through a fiery fen and over a misty moor. It climbed a ruby ridge, flung across a valley of violets, and sped along the pearly path leading to the myriad mazes of the Moonstone Mines.

Twenty hoofs thundered hotly through a haunted hollow of spectral sycamores hung with lighted lanterns and past a turquoise tarn and along an avenue of asphodel that turned and twisted down a dark descent which led at last to a pale and perilous plain. The setting sun sank into the sea, seven stars shone suddenly in the sky, and the white deer's dreadful day was done, its race was run, for now it stood silent and still and shivering under the mighty crag called Centaurs Mountain.

King Clode and the Princes Thag and Gallow prepared to loose their arrows, and Jorn closed his eyes against the sight. When he opened them a moment later, the royal huntsmen had dropped their bows and arrows to the earth to stare, not at a deer at bay, but at a tall and dark and youthful maiden, a veritable princess, clad in a long white satin robe, the sparkle of jewels in her hair, golden sandals upon her feet, her red lips parted prettily, her dark eyes shining.

Four horses raised eight ears in sharp surprise, three Princes fell upon their knees at the maiden's feet, and the King glowered and tugged at his mustaches.

"As royal a run as any king could know," he growled, "and it ends as always in vanished venison and a lovely lady to carry to her kingdom. Pray God her father has a decent taste in wines!"

But when young Jorn, who alone of the Princes could find his tongue, asked the maiden to name her name and

tell her kingdom, she could only shake her head and say she did not know.

King Clode sighed. "Swing her to your saddle, Jorn," he said, "and we will serve her at our table in another way than I had hoped. Make haste before that wicked woods wizard shows up to make sport of us all."

Prince Jorn lifted the Princess to his saddle and the jingle of the harness bells and buckles sounded like merry laughter in King Clode's ears as he whirled his horse about and they began the long ride home across the pale and perilous plain, up the dark descent, along the avenue of asphodel, past the turquoise tarn, through the haunted hollow of spectral syca-

mores hung with lighted lanterns, in and out of the myriad mazes of the Moonstone Mines, along the pearly path, across the valley of violets, over the ruby ridge and the misty moor, through the fiery fen and the golden glade and the bronze bog and the silver swamp, in and out of the flock of wingless birds, across the musical mud, past the barking tree and through the green forest and the shimmering fireflies and out at last upon the open road that led straight to the castle.

THE LOST PRINCESS

The next morning the Princess sat in an eastern room, and watched the sunlight, falling through slits and circles in the ancient castle wall, make small bright patterns on the cold stone floor.

The Royal Wizard, a wizard, as we have said, of meager devices, juggled seven silver spheres for the entertainment of the Princess, while Quondo sat in the corner and watched first the silver spheres and then the dark bewildered eyes of the lovely maiden. She had lain awake most of the night trying in vain to remember her name and the name of her father.

On the floor at her feet, the Royal Recorder sat cross-legged, chanting the names of kings from a ponderous ledger in the hope that one of them might light a light in the lady's eyes. He had reached the P's and droned steadily on. . . . "Paq, Pardo, Payorel, Pent, Perril, Peo, Pilligro, Piv, Podo, Polonel, Puggy." At the name "Puggy," the Princess started slightly—but only because the Royal Wizard had dropped one of the silver spheres. Quondo picked it up and tossed it back to him.

The Royal Recorder made a series of sounds with his tongue and teeth. "King Puggy," he said, disapprovingly, "is the most disreputable king in the whole Registry of Kings. He lives in a ruined castle on a hill with his seven madcap daughters. The old king's wife died of a fit of

shrieks when all the Princesses were very young. Now Puggy and his seven maids live all alone, wreaking every kind of hob and havoc on their hill: rolling boulders down on passersby, turning rivers from their normal course, stealing gems and silks from caravans so they can dress in gawdy masquerade and play their wild and eerie games by jack-o'-lantern light." The Royal Recorder raised his hands and shook his head. "Every night is Hallowe'en on Puggy's Hill."

The Princess frowned and turned a little pale. The Royal Recorder sighed again and read more names, glancing at the Princess after every name, but she gave no sign of recognition. He ran on, through twenty Q's and thirty R's and forty S's and ten T's and five U's and two V's and thirteen W's and ninety X's and fifty-six Y's and came at last to the Z's. "Zar," he said, and the Princess jumped in her chair, but only because the Royal Wizard had dropped another silver sphere. Quondo tossed it back to him and the juggling and the droning continued: "Zazo, Zat, Zawazaw, Zav, Zax, Zay, Zazir, Zazuno, Zyzz," chanted the Recorder, and he closed the record of royalty with a dusty thump, shook his head sadly and stood up.

The Wizard let the silver spheres drop into a wide pocket of his long robe. Quondo gazed softly at the Princess.

"I have a memory of trees and fields and a memory of nothing more," she sighed.

"This presents a problem for a practitioner of physic," said the Royal Recorder, "but unhappily, the Royal Physician is quite ill of some mysterious malady and has given orders that he must not be disturbed." The Princess studied with troubled eyes a pattern of crenelated shadow on the floor. "There is, to be sure, the Royal Clockmaker. He has made several shrewd surmises in his time. Tocko, the Clockmaker," he added, "was formerly the Royal Astronomer." The Princess took her kerchief and wiped a ledger smudge from the Royal Recorder's cheek.

"Why is Tocko no longer the Royal Astronomer?" she asked.

"He got so old he could not see the planets very well, or

24

even the moon or even the sun," said the Recorder. "His constant reports that everything was going out alarmed King Clode, who must have light to hunt by, as you know —and no offense intended."

The Princess smiled faintly.

The Recorder went on. " 'Let me have men in my towers who bring me news of bright sun and stars!' King Clode then cried. So Tocko was set to making clocks and chimes and sundials, and a younger man named Paz now scans the skies. He has invented rose-colored lenses for his telescope so even the palest moon and coldest star turn red and deep, and it is thus reported to the King. Let us visit the shadowy shop of ancient Tocko and hear what we may hear."

They found Tocko in his shop carving a legend on a sundial: "After this brief light, the unending dark." The old

man's eyes were so dim and a hundred clocks ticked and chimed so loudly that he was not aware of his visitors. The Princess read the legend carved on another sundial: "It is darker than you think," and on a third: "This little light and then the night." The Royal Recorder tapped the ancient Clockmaker on his shoulder, and Tocko

looked up with pale and misty eyes.

"I bring a nameless Princess," said the Royal Recorder, "who has a memory of trees and fields and a memory of nothing more." He cupped his hand close to the old man's ear and told the tale of the white deer and of how it had been transformed into a tall and dark and lovely Princess at the foot of Centaurs Mountain, and of how he had read out all the names of kings in the Royal Register without lighting a light in the eyes of the Princess. "You were ever a man of shrewd surmises and gifted guesses," concluded the Royal Recorder. "What say you ails the lady?"

The Clockmaker waved the long thin fingers of one hand. "Send the lady to walk in the gardens," he said, "where the silver fountains play, the while I hazard a few hazards as to what has happened to her head." The hands of the hundred clocks pointed to noon but the clocks chimed eight and six and nine and four and all the other hours but twelve. "Maidens have a strange effect on clocks," said Tocko, "causing them to strike too little or too long, making a travesty of time." The Royal Recorder led the Princess to the door and showed her the gardens where the silver fountains played, and he watched her until she moved among them, lovely but forlorn, beyond the sound of clocks and voices.

"Perhaps she had a fall and struck a stone," said the Recorder, "and in this wise lost her memory." The old man shook his head. "Perhaps she drank a potion or a philter," said the Recorder, "and in this wise lost her memory." The old man shook his head again and said, "You asked *me* to assume assumptions, and you assume assumptions of your own." The Recorder said that he was sorry, and listened in silence while the old man spoke.

"I mind a tale my father told a hundred years ago or thereabouts," said Tocko, "a marvelous tale of a true deer who befriended a woods wizard. It seems this woods wizard in the olden time had a fall or drank a potion or a philter and tumbled senseless in a stream in April when streams are swift and strong. The tale tells how a passing deer plucked the senseless wizard from the stream and saved his life. In return for this good and timely deed, he gave the deer the power of changing to a Princess, tall and dark and lovely, in the event that hunters pressed it hard and there was nowhere to flee, as when a deer is brought to bay at Centaurs Mountain."

The Recorder's eyes grew large and round and his mouth fell open. In the pause that followed, the hundred clocks, whose hands pointed to eleven minutes after noon, struck thirteen times. When the chiming ceased, the Recorder spoke. "Do you mean to tell me, Tocko, that this Princess is in all save shape and semblance a true deer and not a Princess of the royal blood?"

"In due course," pursued the old man, "the deer I speak of in the ancient time was hotly pressed by some hobbledehoy of the region, unaccountably skillful in the saddle, and brought to bay against a crag too steep to climb. As the hunter raised his bow, the panting wild-eyed deer became before his goggling eyes a Princess in all seeming, tall and dark and lovely. The hobbledehoy turned white and red and blue and rode off as fast as his spent horse could travel, leaving his bow and arrow on the ground.

"The deer in maiden's guise made its way to the cave of the woods wizard it had befriended and put to him a quavering question: how could it remain a maiden and live in the manner of a maiden? The wizard, out of his old gratitude, gave the deer the power of remaining a maiden, in shape and semblance, until such time as love should fail her

28

thrice. If love should fail her thrice, then she must resume her true form forever and forever, come what may.

"The first to love her was a poet, the second was a minstrel, the third was a knight. Each in his turn discovered her true nature and each in his turn failed of his love. For who can love a lady who is in reality a deer?"

There was for a long moment only the ticking of the clocks and the faint sound of the fountains.

"And in the end," asked the Royal Recorder, "when love had failed her thrice?"

"In the end, when love had failed her thrice," Tocko said, "she was instantly changed back into her true and proper form. A fortnight later she was hard pressed by the same hobbledehoy who had pursued her before. This time his arrow found her heart."

The clocks all of a sudden struck seven. "Is this a truth you tell me?" demanded the Recorder.

"The white deer of my father's time knew not her name, for wild deer have no names. She had a memory of trees and fields and a memory of nothing more," old Tocko said.

"How can I tell this tale to Clode, the proudest hunter of his day?" the Royal Recorder cried. "I beg you, Tocko, doubt your doubts and hope some hopes this Princess may be real."

The old man coughed. "Against the may, the could be, and the should, folly 'tis to balance doubt or hope. I know the symbols, signs and symptoms of a thousand spells. Sorceries run in cycles."

Neither the old man nor the younger observed a dark form in a gloomy corner of the shop. It was the squatty figure of Quondo who had crept in, unnoticed. His eyes were closed that they might not sparkle and be seen, but he was not asleep. The Royal Recorder turned without a word, opened the heavy oaken door and went out.

He watched the lovely Princess walk toward him, the sparkle of jewels in her hair, golden sandals on her feet, and he marveled that a deer, if this was indeed a deer, could take so perfectly the shining semblance of a lady of royal blood. The Royal Recorder wondered if he could truly love a lady who might at this time or that, depending on the special spell that held her in enchantment, begin to nibble at the young leaves on the trees. He decided with a sigh and a shake of his head that he could not, and made a little note to this effect in the archives of his heart.

There were question marks in the dark eyes of the nameless maid, but the Royal Recorder shook his head and looked away and sighed. "The old man moaned and maundered, murmured, muttered, mumbled odds of this and ends of that, bits and pieces, shreds and edges, full of ifs and whens and theres and thens, amounting in the end and all to six times less than nothing."

He bowed and sighed and bowed again and watched the

Princess cross the grass like summer rain and vanish through a portal.

It was a silent meal that noon in the long banquet hall which was so dark even in the daytime that torches flared from iron sconces on the heavy stone walls. The mysterious maiden ate several walnuts, refused wine, and nibbled at a leaf of lettuce in such a way as to remind the uncomfortable King and his older sons of the previous day in the enchanted forest and their swift and surprising quarry. Clode and Thag and Gallow stirred restlessly in their chairs and grunted now and then. Prince Jorn, whose fond eyes betrayed his feeling for the nameless Princess, was pleased to see that she regarded him softly whenever she raised her own eyes to look down the table. Quondo, the dwarf, once more in his corner under the iron shield, missed no glance or grunt. His dark eyes never left the figures at the table.

"If you do not eat better than this," said the King to the Princess, "I shall have to consult the Royal Gamekeeper. I mean," he hastily corrected himself, "the Royal Physician." The Princess turned a pretty pink, Jorn scowled at his father, and the King, to cover his confusion, bawled for the Royal Wizard, who appeared suddenly in a cloud of smoke.

"I thought I told you not to appear in a cloud of smoke any more," growled the King. "The smell of powder spoils the fragrance of the wine. I told you that."

"I forgot," said the Wizard.

"Just come in the room like anybody else," said the King.

"Yes, Sire," said the Wizard, and he began to juggle seven little crescent moons made of gold and silver.

The King continued to grumble to himself. "Bad enough when he used to appear in a flash of lightning and a clap of thunder. Worse now when he smells up the whole castle. Fellow's foolish tricks do not justify such an elaborate entrance. Average woods wizard knows more in one day than this buffoon learns in ten years, spite of the fact he attended one of the most expensive schools for sorcerers in the world. Bah! Can't teach a man to ride a horse or cast a spell. Comes naturally or it doesn't come at all."

Muttering and pulling at his mustaches, King Clode drank off a goblet of white wine, got up from the table and went up the winding stone stair. He was still talking to himself, and his voice echoed hollowly through castle halls and chambers: "I'll purge this lovely lady of her namelessness or eat an uncooked horse." He listened at the door of the chamber where the Royal Physician lay in bed, alternately groaning and comforting himself:

"I'll never walk again. . . . Come, come, we'll have us out of bed in no time; we'll bring the roses to those cheeks of ours in no time. . . . No, we won't. . . . Yes, we will. . . . No, we won't. . . . Yes, we will."

A long silence followed and the King entered the chamber. The Royal Physician was taking his temperature, but he shook the mercury down without looking at it.

"As a physician, I must take my temperature every three hours," he said, "but as a patient, I must not be told what it is."

"Nobody ever tells *me* what anything is," said the King, who did not know what the Royal Physician was talking about. "I came to speak to you as a physician, not as a patient."

"I do not believe I can cure myself," said the sick man. "Now, now," he retorted to himself, "we mustn't lose faith in the skill of our physician, must we?"

The King sighed and went to a window and looked out on the castle grounds. He tugged at the lobe of his right ear with his left hand and told the tale of the white deer which he and his sons had pursued, and how it had become a tall, dark and lovely Princess who had a memory of trees and fields and a memory of nothing more. When he had finished the tale, he asked the Physician what he thought was wrong with the Princess that she could not remember her name or the name of her father.

"Perhaps she had a fall," said the sick man, in his suave physician's voice, "or perhaps she drank a potion or a philter."

"She has no bruise on her head," said the King, "and the pupils of her eyes are not dilated."

"Hm," said the Royal Physician, "I must study the case

when I get up, if I ever do, which I doubt. Roses in my cheeks, indeed! I don't believe I have the slightest notion what is the matter with me. . . . Come, come, we mustn't get ourself all worked up, must we?"

"I don't know," said the bewildered King. He looked at the sick man, sighed, and left the chamber and went to his couch where he lay thrashing and muttering to himself for an hour. He got up at last and went heavily down the winding stone stair.

In the eastern chamber from which the sunlight had departed, the King found the Royal Wizard juggling the seven little moons and the seven silver spheres by the light of seventeen tall candles. The Royal Recorder was reciting the names of imaginary kings to the Princess, who sat in the same chair she had sat in during the morning when he had recited the names of real kings. "Rango, Rengo, Ringo, Rongo, Rungo," chanted the Recorder. "Rappo, Reppo, Rippo, Roppo, Ruppo."

The Royal Wizard dropped a moon and a sphere and complained that the flickering candlelight made it difficult to see. Quondo squatted in his corner, his dark eyes on the puzzled face of the Princess.

"Santo, Sento, Sinto, Sonto, Sunto," droned the Recorder. "Talatar, Teletar, Tilitar, Tolotar, Tulutar. Undan, Unden, Undin, Undon, Undun."

"What mummery goes forward here in the flickering light?" roared Clode.

"I am making up the names of kings in the hope that one of them may light a light in the eyes of the Princess,"

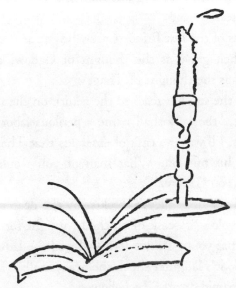

said the Recorder. "Varalare, Veralare, Viralare, Voralare, Vuralare. Waxy, Wexy, Wixy, Woxy, Wuxy," he intoned.

"Pap, Pep, Pip, Pop, Pup!" cried the King in disgust. "Enough of this Wixy, Waxy, Wuxy! The lovely lady may be nameless, but any fool can see she is not the imaginary daughter of an imaginary monarch. I'll solve this pretty problem in the manner of a king, without a lot of this tarradiddle and tirradaddle. I ordain and decree here and now that the Princess shall set a perilous labor for each of my three sons, and the first who succeeds in his task shall marry the wench. Nothing like marriage to bring a woman to her senses."

The eyes of the lost Princess grew bright as she thought of Jorn, then grave as she thought of Gallow, and then frightened as she thought of Thag.

"When the sun has reached the zenith on the morrow," said Clode, "the lady shall name a perilous labor for each of my sons. I'll wager a cask of emeralds that Thag returns first from his mission. What man of you would risk as many gems on Gallow?"

There was a little silence, broken by the deep rumble of Quondo's voice. "A cask of emeralds, weight for weight," he said, "that young Prince Jorn will wed the lady."

King Clode's laughter shook the heavy walls. "Done and done, my stupid dwarf," he bellowed.

The Princess rose, curtsied to the King, and walked from the chamber, followed by Quondo and the Wizard. As King Clode made to go, the Royal Recorder began in a quavering voice: "There is a tale that Tocko tells . . ."

"Tell me no tale that Tocko tells," said the King. "The ancient ass reported comets which in truth were glow-worms. His hundred clocks all chime by chance. He sets his sundials in the shade. Tell me no tale that Tocko tells."

The Royal High Chamberlain entered the room without knocking, and bowed to the King. "The Royal Astronomer, Sire," he said, "seeks an immediate audience. Something has gone amiss in the skies."

"Send him in! Send him in!" shouted Clode. "Don't stand there bowing and nodding your head—send him in!"

The Royal High Chamberlain bowed and nodded and withdrew.

"My father loved this flourish and formality," said Clode. "I see no need for podgy go-betweens. If a man wants to come and see me, let him come and see me."

There was a knock on the door and Paz, the Royal Astronomer, came into the room. He was a young pink-cheeked man in a pink robe and his pink eyes peered through pink lenses.

"A huge pink comet, Sire," he said, "just barely missed the earth a little while ago. It made an awful hissing sound, like hot irons stuck in water."

"They aim these things at me," said Clode. "Everything

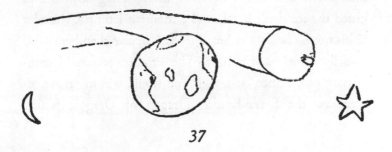

37

is aimed at me." He strode out of the room and slammed the door with such force that all the ledgers flew open and all their leaves fluttered in the wind.

The next day when the sun was at the zenith, the lost lady sat in a high carved golden chair in a great circular chamber reserved for royal ceremonies and commanded each of the three Princes in turn to fall on bended knee before her while the King and the Royal Recorder looked on.

The Princess spoke. "I commission you, Prince Thag, if you would win my hand, to hunt and kill with single lance and all alone, the great Blue Boar of Thedon Grove in the Forest of Jeopardy, and to bring its golden tusks to me and place them at my feet."

"A hundred knights have lost their lives hunting the great Blue Boar of Thedon Grove in the Forest of Jeopardy!" cried Thag.

"Does great Prince Thag hunt nothing more perilous than white deer?" the Princess asked. Thag bowed, and kissed the maiden's hand, and a moment later the thunder of his horse's hoofs was heard in the circular chamber.

Gallow knelt in his turn. The Princess spoke. "I commission you, Prince Gallow, if you would win my hand, to overcome the Seven-headed Dragon of Dragore which guards the Sacred Sword of Loralow, and to bring back the Sacred Sword of Loralow and place it at my feet."

"A hundred knights have lost their lives striving to overcome the Seven-headed Dragon of Dragore!" he cried.

"Does great Prince Gallow hunt nothing more perilous than white deer?" the Princess asked. Prince Gallow bowed, and kissed the maiden's hand, and a moment later the thunder of his horse's hoofs was heard in the circular chamber.

Jorn was the last to kneel. The Princess spoke. "I commission you, Prince Jorn, if you would win my heart and hand, to vanquish the Mok-Mok which guards the cherry trees in the Orchard of Chardor ten leagues from the castle gates, and to bring back a silver chalice filled with a thousand cherries and place it at my feet."

King Clode leaned forward in his great oaken chair. "The Mok-Mok is a creature made of clay and sandalwood constructed by my father's father's father's father three hundred years ago to scare off rocs who used to strip the trees of cherries," he cried.

"A hundred children have carved their names on the dreadful Mok-Mok in the cherry orchard of Chardor!" cried Jorn.

"Does the great Prince Jorn hunt nothing less perilous than white deer?" the Princess asked.

Jorn bowed, and kissed the maiden's hand, and a moment later the thunder of his horse's hoofs was heard in the circular chamber.

The Princess rose, curtsied to the King, and went up the winding stone stair to minister to the Royal Physician and to the Castle Wizard who, in trying to remove his own head and replace it, had succeeded only in straining his neck so that he had taken to his bed.

King Clode walked around the room, absently snapping the shields on the wall with his thumbnail and making them ring. "She has a lovely face," he said. "I like the child. And yet I have the oddest feeling she is watching me in soft alarm, like a creature peering through the underbrush."

The Royal Recorder put his right index finger alongside his nose. "Like a startled fawn, perhaps, trembling in the pussy willows?" he said.

The King whirled on him. "No, not like a startled fawn trembling in the pussy willows!" he snarled. "I slept lightly all night long, hearing every chirp and squeal and hoot and rustle, and something that kept going 'clong!' off in that direction." He pointed a little west of north. "I hear it every night."

"They say the forest wizards bounce things off the moon. It could be that," the Royal Recorder said.

The King sighed. "A thing went ticking through my thoughts a thousand times," he said. "Tick, clong, tick, clong, tick, clong, went the night." He strode toward the Royal Recorder. "What is this tale that Tocko tells?" he demanded.

The Royal Recorder coughed. "The tale that Tocko tells," he said, "is tortuous and tortured. It has its balances, its noes and yesses, its this way, that way, its 'tis and 'tisn't, its can be, can't be, its six of one and half dozen of the other."

"Babble, babble, babble," said the King. "Blither, blither, blither. I have no time or mind for sophistries and riddles. Tocko's tales go round and round and make less sense than whirligigs."

"I'll do my best," the Royal Recorder said, and he told the tale of Tocko's father's deer, putting in a hundred twists and tangents of his own.

The King turned from pink to purple as he listened, and from purple to gray. When at last he found his voice, he croaked, "Pray God our deer is different from Tocko's father's deer."

The Royal Recorder turned up the palms of his hands.
"Sorceries, as Tocko says, run in cycles. To put it another
way, spells are set in sets and systems. What's true of one
peculiar case is true of all peculiar cases of the same peculiar
sort. If some knave had not removed my History of Sorcery
from its proper shelf, I could show you what I mean. The
History was compiled by your father's Recorder, and your
father's Recorder's father, and your father's Recorder's father's father. It has no index and no glossary, and it's both
dog-eared and foxed."

"What's 'foxed'?" asked Clode.

"The History of Sorcery," said the Royal Recorder.
"Aren't you listening?"

"I want to know what 'foxed' means!" bawled Clode.

"Oh, spotted," said the Recorder.

"Oh, 'spotted'!" mimicked the King. "It just happens
that I have the History of Sorcery in my chamber. I've been
reading it at night when I couldn't sleep." He clapped his
hands and a small man in yellow appeared, and Clode in-
structed him to go to the Royal bedchamber and bring
down the History. "Get three men to help you," said Clode.

"Persons removing the History of Sorcery or other vol-
umes from the Royal Library should fill out the proper
form," said the Royal Recorder stiffly.

"I won't be listed and labeled or tabbed and tagged," said
Clode. "If I want a book, I'll get a book."

The King and the Royal Recorder began to pace up and down the room in opposite directions, grunting and sighing, respectively, as they passed each other. Presently four small men in yellow came into the room stooping and staggering under the weight of an ancient and enormous volume on Sorcery. They set it down on the floor and left the room and the Royal Recorder began to turn the yellow dusty pages, squinting and coughing.

"There's nothing under Deer," he said at last, "except the record and report of maidens changed to deer and back again, all nice and neat and normal, all neat and nice and formal. In every single case the disenchanted lady knew her name. It says so here."

"Look under something else then!" roared the King.

"Such as?" the Royal Recorder asked. "For instance and example?"

"Look under Loss of Maidens' Memory!" bawled Clode. "Look under L!"

"Loss in this especial case comes under M," the Royal Recorder said.

"How does and can and could it?" thundered Clode.

The Royal Recorder's voice was prim and firm. "The proper listing, Sire, is, colon, quote, Memory, Maidens', Loss of, stop, unquote."

The King closed his left eye and then opened it and closed his right eye. His voice was low and ominous. "I do

not have the slightest doubt that Pussycat comes under Q
and Monkey-muddle under R and Donkey-daddle under S.
Look up the sorry secret of this nameless child under X or
Y or Z, but look it up!" The shields on the wall trembled.

The Royal Recorder turned to the M's and ran through
Magic, Miracle, Mystery, and Mumps before he found at
last what he was looking for, wedged in between Mice and
Mountebank. The King paced up and down while the Recorder read a dozen pages, exclaiming "ah" and "oh" and
"oh" and "ah" until King Clode shouted, "Stop your
whinkering and read me what it says."

The Royal Recorder shook his head. "You'd just get mad.
It's full of clauses and phrases and pauses, and marginal
notes and inner quotes, and words in Latin and words in
Greek, *viz.* and *ibid.* and *circa* and *sic.*"

"Sum it up, then, sum it up," roared Clode, "in language
workaday and commonplace, without a lot of twaddle-twee
and tweedle-twa."

The Royal Recorder flushed. "We have here under M,"
he said, "the tale of nine enchantments in which a deer of
the woods and fields was changed into a woman."

"Why were they?" demanded Clode.

The Royal Recorder spoke slowly and patiently. "One:
because the deer had saved a wizard's life. Two: because the
wicked wizard wished to play a woeful prank on men."

"If I were King of all the world," said Clode, "I'd make

an end of scorcery or break my backbone in the try. In such confusion and caprice who knows his hound dog from his niece?"

"Two things are true," the Royal Recorder said, "in all these nine enchantments. First, the maidens had no names. They had a memory of trees and fields and a memory of nothing more."

"Hah!" said Clode.

"Moreover, too, and furthermore, the spells were all the same. In every strange and single case herein set down and forth, the deer was chased and closely pressed and had nowhere to flee."

"Ho!" said Clode.

"Whereupon, and then and there, the deer was changed into a maid, a tall and dark and lovely maid, a very Princess to the sight."

"Hoy," groaned Clode and he sat down heavily on a stool.

The Recorder walked up and down and stood still and raised his hand. "These false females, these mock maidens, these will-o'-the-wisp women, these pseudo-Princesses, have one disturbing power in common."

"What power is this?" croaked Clode.

"Love them truly, love them well, nothing then can break the spell." The Royal Recorder paused a moment and then went on. "But if love should fail them thrice, they would vanish in a trice."

Clode jumped to his feet and strode up and down the chamber. "Take an edict," he said at last. The Recorder found ink and a quill behind a cobweb on a shelf and drew a parchment from behind a shield and sat on the floor and crossed his legs. Clode closed his eyes and said, "Write it

plain and write it clear: No son of mine shall wed a deer."

"A deer in any form or figment," said the Royal Recorder, "or guise or get-up, or shape or seeming, or image or effigy, or mockery or make-believe—"

"Who's issuing this edict?" demanded Clode.

The Recorder's voice was flat and firm. "It's far too clear," he said. "It should be writ in such a way that if you ever changed your mind, the point could be disowned, denied and disavowed."

"Erase the edict," said the King. He looked sad for a moment, and then guffawed. "Our quandary has its sorrowful side indeed, yet half my kingdom would I give to see the face of Thag, the second huntsman of his time, waking to behold on the pillow next to his, the day the spell is broken, not raven locks and ruby lips but hairy ears and velvet nostrils!"

The force of the King's laughter caused him to bounce from wall to wall of the chamber like a ball in a box. His laughter and his bouncing increased as he thought of Gallow, and then of Jorn, face to face with the lady in her true form and substance, a creature of the fen and not the fireside, the bog, not the boudoir, the salt lick, not the silver bowl.

The King controlled himself long enough to say, "The thing that most amuses me in all this farce and fantasy's the thought of Jorn, Jorn of the lute and lyre, discovering he has won the heart and hoof of the swiftest deer in Christendom." He sat down on a chair and rubbed the tears of merriment from his eyes. The Royal Recorder took a turn across the chamber and back again, stirring the candle flames. Clode sighed three times. "The damsel has lighted lights inside my heart—there's no denying that," he said. "I wish I could decree she never *was* a deer."

"You can't do that," said the Royal Recorder.

"What can I do?" asked Clode.

"Wait and see what you shall see and watch what you shall watch, remembering that one is once and two is twice and three is thrice, and swifter than the twinkling is the trice."

"Yammer, yammer, yammer," said the King. "I've had my fill of yammering. We must advise this Princess she's a deer. Perhaps she'll have the grace to disappear."

"She can't do that," the shocked Recorder said. "By your decree the creature set a set of perils for your sons. She now awaits the swiftest one. The thing is simply done and done."

"I thought she was a Princess at the time," said Clode.

The Royal Recorder shrugged. "Insofar and inasmuch as your decree has made her such, she *is* a Princess, Sire," he said. *"De Facto* and *Pro Tem."*

The King raised his head and gave the great "Harrooo" of a lion tortured by magical mice. He strode so heavily to the door that the shields jangled on the wall. "I hope that all my sons get lost," said Clode. "That's one way out."

"It is for them," the Royal Recorder said, "but not for you. You'd have the pretty creature on your hands until the day that great dark planet Tocko saw goes bump against the world and kills us all."

King Clode sighed, and scowled, and snarled: "That was no great dark planet Tocko saw, but just a falling leaf or flying bird. Why must good King Clode be plagued by blind buffoons and dusty clowns and all the wicked wizards in the world?"

He rushed out of the room and slammed the door with

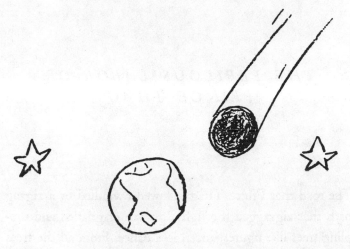

such force that the wind blew the Royal Recorder flat on his face on the floor.

THE PERILOUS LABOR OF
PRINCE THAG

The road that Prince Thag followed dwindled to a zigzag path that zigzagged through a growth of gnarled and toppling trees like figures frozen in a dance. From all the trees a sticky thickish liquid dripped and oozed and gave or rather lent the air a heavy sweetish fragrance, for the sweetish heavy fragrance died and rose and died again and rose and died and rose again.

"This heavish sweety fragrance," Thag muttered to himself, "that rises, or that roses, isn't fit for human noses, and it tricks the minds of men. Three times two is eight," he said, "and one is ten."

A furry bluish smoke came drifting through the trees in rings and hoops and collars.

"I distrust this stickish thicky stuff—" The tall Prince bit his lip. "Hag's thad enough."

"A lozy moon globbers in the pipe trees," said a voice in a tone which for one reason or another thaggravated Had.

"I'm up here in the crouch of the tree," the voice continued.

"Crotch, you mean," said Thag, catching sight of a roundish balding man a few feet above him.

"On the contrary," said the man, "crunch is what you meet in aching."

"That's wince," said Thag angrily.

"Mince is what you do to words," the round man retorted.

"It's glibbers, in any case," said Thag haughtily, "not globbers, as you said. The word is in the pleasant trense."

"Ah, but you speak of mood," said the round man. "I was referring to the moon. It is important to mind your D's

and N's in these particular woods, which are not *too* particular, if you grasp *me*."

"Nobody's grabbing *you*," said Thag. He showed his
upper teeth. "Furthermore, I resent your preferring to it
as a 'peasant trench.' "

The other stared down at Thag. "I don't care what you
say," he said coldly. "I say glibbers."

High up in a tree, a chock climbed slowly.

"I wonder what type it is?" said Thag.

"It's sick thirsty," said the man, "or half past hate or a
quarter to fight. I'm in no moon for questions."

"You're in no *mood*," said Thag.

"First he accosts me, then he tells me what I'm not in,"
said the man. "I crutch in the crouch of this tree to avoid
troublemakers like you, riding on their nagamuffins."

"You are thinking of ragmudgeons," said Thag with
dignity.

"Now he tells me what I'm thinking of," said the man.

"And crouch is what you do, not where you are," said
Thag.

"How can I do anything where I am not?" asked the
man. "I have half a mind to come down and trounce you."

Thag laughed.

"That's right," whined the man, "laugh at a man with
only half a mind." He sniffled. "A man with a crutch."

"You crouch in a crotch, but you have no crutch," said Thag.

The man burst into tears. "That's right," he bawled, "laugh at a man because he has no crutch." He shook his fist at Thag and cried, "A plague on both your horses!"

Four redbirds in a tangle bush sang "verti verti verti go"

as Thag closed his mouth and held his breath and shut his eyes and galloped on through the stingish ringy smoke and the trickish sicky smell, and after a long moment he rode out of the growth of gnarled and toppling trees, and beheld before his eyes the shining Valley of Euphoria.

The air sparkled with the high fine sparkle of crystal which made the three men who approached Thag seem larger than they really were. The three men stood beside Thag's horse and bowed and smiled and bowed. Thag saw that each man held in his hand a mask exactly like his face, but the first mask was stern, the second mask was sad and the third mask was solemn. The first man giggled, the second man chuckled, and the third man chortled. The first man bowed and spoke. "We wear our masks on yesterdays and on tomorrows."

The second said, "And since those sad days never come—"

The third man said, "We know no sorrows." He waved his mask at Thag. "My name is Wag, and this is Gag and that is Jag."

"My name," said Thag, "is Thag."

"A lovely name," said Wag.

"A charming name," said Gag.

"A truly gorgeous name," said Jag. "I wish I'd thought of it myself."

"Welcome to Euphoria," said Wag, "the sweetest little land in all the world, a hundred million welcomes, Thag. You are the finest, greatest Prince that we have ever known."

"You do not know me well," said Thag.

"We know you perfectly," said Wag.

"We know you wonderfully," said Gag.

"We know you beautifully," said Jag.

Thag frowned. "I seek the way to Thedon Grove in the Forest of Jeopardy," he said. "I must ride on. My time is short."

"Jeopardy's so far away you'll never reach it in a day," said Wag.

"Or in a month," said Gag.

"Or in a year," said Jag. "We know the place, a truly gorgeous place."

"A charming place," said Gag.

"A lovely place," said Wag.

Thag grew restless on his restless horse. "Tell me, are the perils worse, and have the monsters grown?"

The three men placed their arms about each other's shoulders and laughed until they cried and cried until they laughed again.

"The perils and the monsters," giggled Wag, "are neither here nor there nor anywhere."

"Forget the perils," chuckled Gag.

"Dismiss the monsters," chortled Jag.

The three men laughed and cried again and cried and laughed.

"Which way to Jeopardy?" yelled Thag in such a voice the laughter and the crying stopped.

"It's straight ahead," said Wag.

"Ride by the Bye," said Gag.

"And pass the Time of Day," said Jag.

The three men began to giggle and chuckle and chortle again as Thag galloped away and straight ahead and on and on through the green Valley which was loud with the sound of gaiety and joy and jollity and frolic and frivolity.

He rode by the Bye, a merry sparkling stream, and passed the Time of Day, a great clock on whose dial was painted a laughing face. The hills fell away on either side and the

grass changed from green to brown and then to gray. A jolly man at the far end of the Valley of Euphoria cried *"Carpe Diem"* as Thag flashed by.

The road was rough and rocky now, geese gaggled by, and thorns fell from the thorn trees and stuck point-down in the earth like daggers. As Thag drew near the edge of Jeopardy, the weather underwent a fearful change. There was a mist of moss to ride through and a storm of glass. Hurricanes and monsoons and tidal waves came in from the sea, tornadoes and cyclones tore up the crust of the earth, and mistrals descended from the mountains.

There was the musical stream to swim, whose soft waters swayed so somnolently and sang so sweetly that Thag had to struggle savagely against drowsiness and death by drowning. His black horse whinnied with fear, but the King's son urged him on and the horse galloped through the perilous woods. A great wind came up from the earth. Trees fell before the horse and rider and behind them and on both sides of them. Great holes opened and closed in the earth like giants' mouths, but Thag guided his horse around them and over them and between them.

Fire swept the forest but Thag sped through it safely. Hailstones as large as chalices fell all around but he avoided them. Lightning flashed and thunder rolled and the rain came down in torrents but Prince Thag rode on, singing.

At last the black trees of Thedon Grove loomed up, the

57

haunt of the great Blue Boar. Thag dismounted, lance in hand, and crept forward cautiously. His ears were deafened by a terrible sound, the sound of snoring, rising and falling. Gripping his lance tightly, Thag moved toward the sound, which seemed to come from the foot of an obob tree. To Prince Thag's high astonishment, the enormous Blue Boar of Thedon Grove, which slept only thirty winks in every thirty years, was snoring under the obob tree, his great eyes closed, his huge sides heaving.

Thag stepped forward softly and swiftly, but the monster, dreaming of danger, opened one eye and struggled to its feet with a mighty *"scarooooof!"*

It was too late. Thag's lance was on its sure way to the Blue Boar's heart. The Blue Boar of Thedon Grove toppled

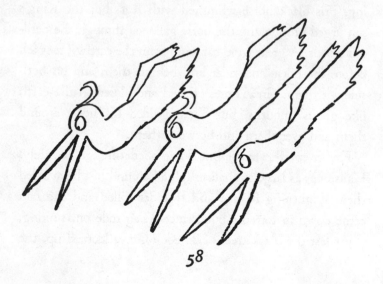

58

over on his side with such force that he dug his own grave. Thag reached down and broke off the golden tusks as easily as if they had been icicles. A moment later he was riding back through the menacing woods.

Round rocks ten feet in diameter crossed and crissed and crisscrossed his path, and buzbuz birds in vast numbers flew at Thag's head, opening and closing their scissor-like beaks. The Prince and his black charger evaded the boulders and the buzbuz birds with marvelous jumps and dodgings, and broke at last into the clear, and raced for the castle of his father, the golden tusks of the great Blue Boar shining in his hand.

From a tall window in a high room of King Clode's castle, the Princess watched with wide eyes and trembling body the road her suitors had taken, to where it split into separate directions like a branching candlestick. Thag had followed the road to the right, Gallow the road to the left, and Jorn had traveled straight ahead.

As far as the mysterious maiden's eyes could see, there was no cloud of dust on any road, no sign of horse or man. She watched the middle road with hope and eagerness, the roads that branched to right and left with terror and dismay.

In his shadowy shop Tocko sat quietly, trying to think

of chill and fragile rhymes for "time" and "sorrow."

The Royal Wizard squatted on the floor of his room in a tower, trying to change a piece of common field stone into gold by wiggling his fingers at it and crying "Ixxyzo!" Nothing happened.

The Royal Physician, still lying in bed, insulting and reassuring himself, tried to stick out his tongue far enough to see whether or not it was coated. "Come, come," he said. "We can stick our tongue out farther than that, can't we?" he asked cheerily. "No, we can't," he replied, sullenly.

In the Royal Library the Royal Recorder sat on a tall stool at a high desk and made an entry in his private diary: "On this day it has been established, despite the fussing and fretting and bawling and moaning of You Know Who, that the so-called Princess we have been entertaining in the castle since the night before last is, in truth and fact, by birth and destiny, a common deer. The discovery of the sorrowful secret of the unhappy beast was made by me."

King Clode sat all alone at the head of the long table in the banquet hall, cracking walnuts between his thumb and forefinger and meditating on the advisability of taking a little wine before visiting the Princess to acquaint her with her pitiful plight. He decided it would not be a good idea to call for wine, and went on cracking walnuts.

As he turned the dilemma over in his mind, his eyes brightened and darkened and brightened and darkened. He cracked his last walnut and ate it slowly, shell and all, and slapped the table with his hand and the silver bowl that had held the walnuts jumped off the table and cackled on the floor. "Steward!" bawled Clode. "Wine!"

High up in a leafy tree where he could not be seen, Quondo scanned the three roads that led to peril. By turning his head to the left and peering through the leaves, he could see the Princess standing at the tall window in the high room.

In the Royal Gamekeeper's lodge, the Royal Gamekeeper's wife rearranged crocks on a shelf, talking to the Royal Gamekeeper over her shoulder. "I don't believe a word of it, I don't care what you say. She never *was* a deer, if you ask me. They made the story up, to cloak their goings-on. You men are all alike. Enchanted Princess, indeed! Enchanted hussy! I know her kind. She loitered in the woods and waved at them!"

The Royal Gamekeeper's wife picked up a crock, rubbed it vigorously with a cloth and set it down again. "Dainty, you insist she is. *I* say she's dirty. And as for being twenty-one, she's nearer thirty." The Gamekeeper's wife wiped and wiped and wiped another crock. "That castle surely needs a woman's hand. It's full of broken glass and spider webs. Too bad Her Royal Highness had to die, poor thing. I always say he struck her in his cups."

She stepped back from the shelf and regarded her handi-work.

"If she *is* a princess then I have no doubt she's one of old King Puggy's daughters—eldest of the seven, I should say. She's pretty in their bold and brazen way. . . . Well, what's the matter? . . . Has the leopard got your tongue?"

The Royal Gamekeeper did not answer. He was sitting in a chair, his hands folded on his stomach, fast asleep.

THE PERILOUS LABOR OF
PRINCE GALLOW

Prince Gallow's way led to the left and then to the right
and then to the left again, and he came at last to a white
path through a peaceful wood. As he jingled along the path,
Gallow stared in amazement at a kind of forest he had
never seen before. The trees were hung with signs and
legends . . . "Lost Babes Found." "Giants Killed While
You Wait." "7 League Boots Now 6.98." "Let Us Waken
Your Sleeping Beauty." "We Put You on an Urn, Men
Put You on a Pedestal." "Consult Panting & Young."
"Seek Grailo, Even Better Than the True Grail." "Coach
Pie, Pumpkin Wheels, Horse Traps, Mice Shoes."

The sign that most interested the gaping Gallow read:
"Visit the Seven-headed Dragon of Dragore. Free, Except
Moondays and Feydays."

As Gallow gazed about in wild wonder, a man wearing
a silver cap and a garment made of brass saluted him.

"Your parchments, brother," said the man in metal.

"I am not your brother, and my name is Prince Gallow," said the perplexed Prince.

"In the Forest of Willbe all men are brothers," the man said.

"This sounds friendly but confusing," said Gallow. "I have no parchments, brother."

The man looked grave for a moment, then closed one eye and spoke in a low voice. "You have the semblance of a gentleman of intelligence and wit," he said. "Now it just happens that I have an extra set of proper parchments that I will let you have for a song."

"What song shall I sing?" said Gallow.

"In the Forest of Willbe a song is three large emeralds," the man replied. "Have you three large emeralds?"

From a sack on his saddle, Gallow extracted three emeralds and gave them to the man, who thereupon handed the Prince a red parchment, a blue parchment, and a white parchment.

"Give the red parchment to the man in white, the blue parchment to the man in red, and the white parchment to the man in blue," he said. "It's less simple that way for everybody." The man in metal touched a finger to his cap and walked away.

Gallow rode along the edge of the woods until he came to another path and he rode down the path until he came to a man in white.

Gallow gave the man in white the red parchment. "Will you point me the way that leads to the Seven-headed Dragon of Dragore?" asked the Prince. The man in white was staring at the red parchment.

"This is not a true and proper parchment," said the man

in white. "The seal is missing, the signature is doubtful, and the symbol is yesterday's." He was grave for a moment, then he closed one eye and spoke in a low voice. "You have the semblance of a gentleman of courage and nobility," he said. "You journey on a mission of high peril, or I am dressed in green. Now I could tear this parchment up, and let you pass, and make no cross for you there on that tree to show a knight has gone this way, but that's too safe for your discomfort and for mine. I'll change the seal and signature and symbol to make the parchment proper, and all this for a song, brother, all this for a song. It's more perilous that way for everybody."

Prince Gallow sighed and gave the man three emeralds from his sack and rode on till he came to the man in blue.

The man in blue took the white parchment and was grave for a moment. Then he closed one eye and spoke in a low voice.

"You have the semblance of a man of learning and discernment, brother," he said, "but I can't let you pass until you prove your power to read, and how can you or I or anyone read this?" He gave the parchment back to Gallow, who saw that the writing on it could be read only by holding it up to a mirror.

"I cannot read these words unless I have a looking-glass," Prince Gallow cried.

The man in blue produced from his sleeve a silver and ivory mirror, and handed it to the frowning Prince. "Now read the legend in the glass," he said.

Gallow tucked the parchment under his chin, held the mirror before him and read: "Forget the Past, Enjoy the Present, the Future Will Take Care of Itself."

Prince Gallow let the parchment drift to the ground. "I have a strange feeling that I am neither Here nor There," he said, "and that this is neither Now nor Then. I am caught somewhere between the day before yesterday and the day after tomorrow."

The man in blue looked grave for a moment. "That is because you have ridden out of the Past into the Future," he said. He closed one eye. "In giving up Was for Willbe, you have lost Am." He spoke in a low voice. "You have had the Past, you behold the Future about you, but you have no Present. Now it just happens that you hold in your hand a very fine present—a present of ivory and silver fit for a princess. Vulcan made it for Venus who left it to Cleopatra who gave it to Isolde who bequeathed it to my grandmother. I will let you have it for a song."

Prince Gallow sighed, drew three emeralds from his sack and gave them to the man in blue.

"Which way to the Seven-headed Dragon of Dragore that guards the Sacred Sword of Loralow?" he asked patiently.

"Turn right, then right, then right, then right," said the man in blue.

"But that would take me around in a square and bring me back to where I am now," said Gallow.

"It's much more impressive that way for everybody," said the man in blue as he walked away, clicking his emeralds.

The second son of Clode rode around the square of paths as he had been directed, and when he came back to where he had started from, he found a man in red waiting for him.

"Your blue parchment," said the man in red. Gallow handed him the parchment.

"Which way to the Seven-headed Dragon of Dragore

that guards the Sacred Sword of Loralow?" the Prince inquired.

The man in red looked grave for a moment; then he closed one eye and spoke in a low voice.

"You have the semblance of a gentleman of shrewdness and cunning," he said. "Close your eyes, brother." Gallow closed his eyes and the man in red concealed the blue parchment under a stone. "Open your eyes, brother," he said, and Gallow opened his eyes. "Do you see the blue parchment that I hold in my hand?" asked the man. "No, you do not, for I have made it invisible. In the same manner I can make you and your horse invisible so that you can ride up to the Seven-headed Dragon of Dragore and take the Sacred Sword of Loralow without being seen. This service I will perform for three songs."

Gallow took nine emeralds from his sack, which left him only twelve, and gave them to the man in red.

"You are invisible now and neither man nor dragon can see you," said the other. "It is more deceptive that way for everybody."

"Which way to the Seven-headed Dragon of Dragore?" demanded Gallow.

"The Hard Way," said the man in red. "Down and down, round and round, through the Moaning Grove of Artanis."

"How shall I know this Grove?" asked Gallow.

"By its red roses and its million moons and its blue houses, in each of which sits a solitary maiden moaning for her lover who is far away. Fear not the roaring of the dreadful Tarcomed, nor yet the wuffing-puffing of the surly Nacilbuper, but ride straight on."

"And when I have passed through the Grove?" asked the Prince.

"Turn to the right and follow a little white light," said the man in red as he walked away, jiggling his emeralds.

Gallow rode and rode till he came to the Grove of Artanis. The scent of the red roses assailed his nostrils, the light of the million moons blinded his eyes, and the moaning of the lonely maidens deafened his ears so that he galloped as fast as his horse could go until he came to a winding road

69

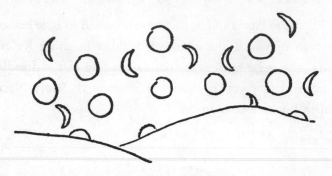

and turned to the right. In front of him appeared suddenly a little white light and he followed it round and round and down and down.

Presently Prince Gallow heard the sound of many people talking and laughing and shouting and singing, and he saw tables along the side of the road spread with fruits and meats, and other tables piled with baubles and gewgaws and gimcracks and kickshaws new to his sight and strange to his memory.

On the trees hung heavy musical instruments he had never dreamed of, and the people were dressed in a remarkable fashion and danced in a remarkable way, down and down and round and round. Above the sounds of the people rose a curious and alarming buzzing and whirring and ringing and thumping.

"Here you are, brother!" cried a man dressed in black and blue, and he held out seven small spheres to Gallow.

"Seven balls for twelve emeralds! Try your luck!"

"You hand me these spheres," said Gallow in a puzzled tone, "yet you cannot see me for I have been made invisible."

"Of course I see you," said the man. "Plain as day, big as life, ugly as sin. Buy the balls and toss them in."

"I do not understand what you are saying," said the bewildered Prince.

"Look, brother," said the man. "Twelve emeralds get you seven balls. You throw the balls at the Seven-headed Dragon of Dragore in that striped tent yonder—the greatest mechanical wonder of the age, meaningless but marvelous. The seven heads go round and round and down and down. Try your luck, try your skill! Toss a ball into each of the seven heads and you win the genuine and only Sacred Sword of Loralow. A ball in six, two golden bricks. Five and dandy, a box of candy. Four a key and three a rose. And so it goes and so it goes."

The man gave the seven balls to Gallow and took his sack of emeralds. "You can't win, brother," he said, "and I can't lose. That makes it fair and square for everybody." He looked grave for a moment, then closed one eye and spoke in a low voice.

"You have the semblance of a gentleman of honor and integrity," he said. "Now if the great key in the side of the mechanical Dragon is not wound, the seven heads will not go round and round and down and down, and you can toss a ball into each of the seven heads and win the Sacred Sword. In return for this little service and secret, I ask only for the golden saddle I see there on your horse."

Gallow was so confused he could not say a word. He strode silently into the striped tent and there he saw the Seven-headed Dragon, its heads now motionless, their mouths open. Between the claws of its great feet lay the glittering sword for which he had endured so much. One after another Gallow tossed the balls until each had dropped into a separate gaping mouth. Then he walked over and picked up the Sacred Sword of Loralow and left the striped tent. As he did so, a small tired man appeared, walked to an iron chest, opened it, took out one of a hundred identical swords and placed it between the paws of the mechanical Dragon. He yawned and shuffled away.

Outside the striped tent the man in black and blue waved gaily at Gallow as the Prince mounted the bare back of his black horse and rode off swiftly the way he had come, up the winding road, past the little white light, through the Grove of Artanis and along the many paths until at last he broke out of the Forest of Willbe and galloped for the castle of his father, the Sacred Sword of Loralow shining in his hand.

The Princess, standing at the tall window in the high room of King Clode's castle, strained her eyes and held her hand to her wild heart. She tried to pray, but since she had a memory of trees and fields and a memory of nothing more, she found no prayer to say.

The Princess tried again to remember her name and she could not. A black doubt crept into her mind and heart. Perhaps she was in truth a nameless waif, a woman of the fields or kitchen, changed into a deer by some woods or castle wizard whom she had unwittingly offended while milking a cow or serving broth. If so, it might have been the wicked wizard's whim to cast a spell that only a king's three sons, in hot pursuit, could break. Perhaps the sorcerer had laughed and said, "Three sons of a famous king will break your spell and break their hearts and then your own, for who would have a milkmaid for his bride?"

Perhaps the true disenchantment would come when the swiftest Prince should place his trophy at her feet and cry, "I claim your heart and hand."

Perhaps then she herself could and would confess, "My name is Such-and-Such and I'm a peasant," or, "My name is So-and-So and I'm a scullery maid." She hoped, if this were to be the awful ending of her cruel enchantment, that Thag or Gallow and not Jorn would be the first to cry, "I

73

claim your heart and hand."

But in spite of these dark thoughts, the eyes of the nameless maiden peered down the straight road Jorn had taken. Shadows lay across the road, spreading and thickening like

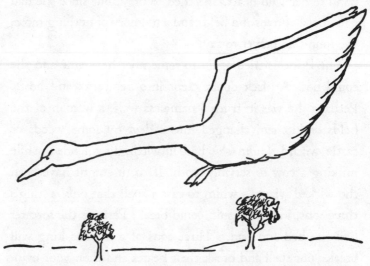

black blood, but there was no sign of dust, no mark of horse or man. The Princess forced herself to look to the left and then to the right. Nothing moved except the shadows of trees stirring in the wind along the road Gallow had taken, but the Princess almost cried out when she saw what she thought was a cloud of dust on the road Thag had followed. It rose slowly above the trees and she saw that it was only a swan flying. The Princess placed her hands over her eyes and shivered.

THE PERILOUS LABOR OF
PRINCE JORN

The way to the cherry orchard lay straight and smooth as a legend for Prince Jorn, with only a small twist here and a little jog there. The sun shone warmly, the wind blew softly, a cock crowed and children called far away, and overhead the birds sang.

In one place a storm of paper cut in the fragilely beautiful designs of snowflakes blew dreamily across the road, and in another a wolf raised his head and howled, enabling Jorn to see that the creature wore a collar.

The youngest son of King Clode rode sorrowfully on his mission in spite of his love for the Princess, for he did not believe the labor set for him held perils worthy of his strength and courage.

"Any child can pluck a thousand cherries and place them in a silver chalice," he said aloud. "Any moon-crazed idiot could overthrow the artificial Mok-Mok, made of clay and sandalwood to frighten birds away. I would meet the Blue

Boar face to face or slay the dreadful dragon with the seven heads. Set me a difficult riddle, a terrible task, a valiant knight to overthrow!"

As Prince Jorn ended his plaint, he heard a voice calling high and shrill. He looked all about him but he could see

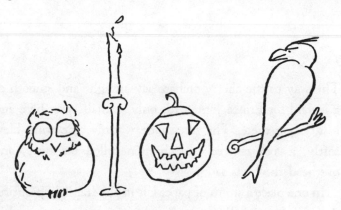

no one, and still the voice kept crying, "Help me, help me, Jorn, and you shall have a difficult riddle, a terrible task, and a valiant knight to overthrow. Help me, help me, Jorn!"

The Prince looked left and right and north and south and down and up, and when he looked up, he saw her— a witch caught on the highest branch of a tree, crying piteously, a witch hung high in the air like a smoky lantern.

Prince Jorn dismounted and climbed the tree and lifted the witch from the highest branch and carried her safely to the ground.

"I was riding the whirlwind," she said, "and got caught in the tree and lost my broom and woe was me."

Jorn looked all around and realized at last that the witch's broom must have fallen into a clump of tall plants called witches'-broom because they look so much like a witch's broom. It took him a long time to find the witch's broom in the witches'-broom but he stumbled on it at last and returned it to its owner.

"For your kindness, Prince Jorn," said the witch as she mounted her broom, "you shall have a difficult riddle to do, a terrible task to undergo, a valiant knight to overthrow." She waved her long bony fingers and sailed away, her shrill laughter trailing behind her.

Jorn rode along the straight smooth way until he came to where a Sphinx crouched beside the road.

"Name me a riddle, Sphinx," said Jorn.

The stony eyes of the Sphinx stared straight ahead and its stony jaws did not move but it spoke:

> *"What is whirly?*
> *What is curly?*
> *Tell me, what is pearly early?"*

Jorn replied in a trice:

> *"Gigs are whirly,*
> *Cues are curly*
> *And the dew is pearly early."*

He rode on a little way and then rode back.

"What was difficult about that riddle?" asked the Prince.

"It was difficult to say without moving my jaws," said the Sphinx.

Jorn shrugged his shoulders and continued on his way until he came all of a sudden upon the great cherry orchard. He dismounted, unslung the silver chalice from his saddle and strode into the orchard, the chalice in his left hand, his sword in his right.

In a clearing in the middle of the cherry orchard lay the Mok-Mok, on its left side. The winds had blown it over, the rains had crumbled its clay, and the worms had eaten its sandalwood. The head of the Mok-Mok had broken off in its fall and larks nested in the hollow eyes. An enormous roc perched drowsily on the shattered monster's flank, and Jorn drove it off with the point of his sword. Not far away in a rusting suit of armor lay the dusty bones of a knight

who had died of terror in the days when the Mok-Mok had been new and awful to look upon.

Jorn saw that the branches of all the trees hung close to the ground under the weight of the bright red fruit they bore, and he wondered that cherries could be so heavy. He dropped his sword in the grass. First with one hand and then with both, he tried to pull a cherry from its stem to put it in the silver chalice, and discovered that it was not a cherry at all, but a ruby in the shape of a cherry. All the cherries on all the trees were rubies and none of them would come off the stems no matter how hard he tugged, and none of the stems would come off the branches.

"You must count a thousand thousand to pick a thousand cherries," said a voice behind Jorn, and the Prince turned to see a small man in a peaked hat looking at him, his large eyes twinkling.

"Say one, two, three," said the man.

"One, two, three," said Jorn.

"Four, five, six," said the man.

"Four, five, six," said Jorn, and when he had counted rapidly up to a thousand, a ruby fell into the silver chalice.

"But a thousand thousand is a million," said Jorn, "and to count to a million is a terrible task!"

"A terrible task you wished for, a terrible task you have," said the man.

Jorn counted to a thousand again, and again a ruby fell into the chalice.

"One, two, three, four, I came to pick cherries, five, six, seven, eight, and I find rubies, nine, ten!" cried Jorn.

"Rubies, cherries, cherries, rubies," said the small man, "it is the same thing."

"Eleven, twelve, how is it the same thing?" asked Jorn. "Thirteen, fourteen, fifteen, sixteen."

The small man paced up and down and said, "What am I doing?"

"Seventeen, eighteen, nineteen, twenty, you are walking back and forth," said Jorn. "Twenty-one—"

"But how can I walk back and forth without first walking forth and back?"

"It is the same thing," said Jorn. "A man who walks, twenty-two, forth and back, twenty-three, is walking back and forth, twenty-four, twenty-five, twenty-six, twenty-seven, twenty-eight, twenty-nine, thirty."

"If forth and back are back and forth, then back is forth and forth is back," said the small one.

"I do not see how that helps me in this terrible task," said Jorn. He finished counting his third thousand and a third cherry dropped into the silver chalice. "At this slow pace Thag will ride home ahead of me with the golden

tusks of the great Blue Boar, and Gallow will ride home ahead of me with the Sacred Sword of Loralow, and one of them will marry the Princess while I still count cherries into my chalice. One, two, three, four, five."

The small man sat on the ground and looked at the Prince and listened as he counted to his fourth thousand and the fourth cherry fell into the silver chalice. Jorn began to count again.

"Fifty princes in fifty years have come to this orchard to gather cherries or rubies for this princess or that," said the small man, "and not one of them has used logic in his labor. I am not a prince and I cannot make the cherries fall —or the rubies, if you will. I have let the other fifty princes pluck the fruit or the jewels their own way because it is worth counting to a million for the heart and hand of a lovely lady. With you, my friend, we have this Thag to think of and this Gallow. There is a logical secret to the falling of the cherries. I cannot tell it outright but I can ask you questions."

"Three hundred and forty-eight, three hundred and forty-nine, three hundred and fifty," said Jorn. "What questions would you ask?"

"Does a cherry drop when you say ninety-nine?"

"No."

"Does a ruby fall when you say nine hundred and ninety-nine?"

"No."

"When does a cherry or a ruby fall?"

"Three hundred and fifty-one. When I say one thousand," said Jorn.

A ruby dropped into his silver chalice.

"One thousand!" cried Jorn again and another ruby fell.

"One thousand, one thousand, one thousand, one thousand!" cried Jorn and four more rubies fell into the chalice.

In no time at all or, to be exact, in one-thousandth the time it would have taken him to count to a million by ones, Jorn had filled the chalice with a thousand rubies. He looked around to thank the small man in the peaked cap, but he was nowhere to be seen. Instead there stood before

Jorn a knight in black armor, the tallest and strongest Black Knight that the young Prince had ever seen.

"Name me your name, Black Knight!" cried Jorn.

"I am Duff of the Dolorous Doom!" thundered a great voice under the gleaming casque which covered all save the dark eyes of the Black Knight. "Fifty princes have I fought beneath these trees, and live to tell the tale!"

Jorn put down the silver chalice and picked up his sword.

"I am armored all in steel. Sets not the balance in my favor?" rumbled the Black Knight.

Jorn raised his sword.

The Black Knight kept his own sword at his side. "There's magic here, I warn you, Prince. What's mightier than magic?"

"Miracle."

"What's miracle?" asked the Black Knight.

"Love's miracle enough."

"Armor, Prince, is stronger stuff." The Black Knight raised his sword swiftly and steel rang against steel. Duff swung his sword above his head with both hands as a man swings an ax, and brought it down so savagely that it whined in the air, but Jorn stepped quickly to one side and thrust at a chink he detected in the Black Knight's armor, just under the right shoulder.

Duff brought up his sword barely in time to strike Jorn's sword away. Time and again he lunged and swung and thrust, and time and again Jorn parried the lunges and side-stepped the swinging steel, stabbing at the chink in Duff's armor whenever it gaped open. Once when a lightning-thrust threw Jorn off balance, the Black Knight would have cleft his head to his chin had he not in turn been thrown

off balance by stumbling against the chalice of rubies, scattering them in the green grass. The battle surged and circled in and out among the trees with a great ringing and flashing of steel. The point of Jorn's sword struck like a bright snake at the chink in the Black Knight's armor which opened and closed like a small mouth as he lunged and drew back and lunged again. The Black Knight began to breathe harder and harder, his thrusts were slower and slower and he no longer lifted the sword high over his head for the cruel slashing strokes which in the first hour of the battle had fallen close to Jorn's body.

At last the Black Knight raised his sword above his head with both hands for a stroke that would cut the young Prince in two like an apple, and swift as light, Jorn's sword darted for the chink under the right shoulder. His sword point cut deep and the Black Knight's weapon fell to the ground. His right arm swung uselessly by his side like a pendulum.

The massive figure in black steel staggered and fell to the grass with a great clangor. The casque that had hidden all save the dark eyes of the Black Knight was wrenched loose and rolled over and over, stopping with a clank against the silver chalice. Prince Jorn saw to his amazement and horror that the head and face revealed to him were the head and face of a man of seventy years. Jorn knelt beside his fallen foe in sorrow and regret and held the knight's head in his arms.

"I would not have fought so venerable a knight had I known," said Jorn.

"You fought the fearful thing I seemed to be, and that's the test and proof of valor, that's the proof and test. When all is dark within the house, who knows the monster from the mouse?" The Black Knight's voice no longer thundered but was small and thin.

Jorn helped the old man to his feet and staunched the

blood and bound his wound. "What may I trust?" cried Jorn. "What's there to trust?"

"Ah, trust your heart," the old man said. "Trust love. Fifty years ago I undertook a fearful labor for a lady's love. Armored all in pride and arrogance, I sought to meet the

dreadful Mok-Mok face to face and came upon this harmless thing of wood and clay. 'Then love's a whim!' I cried, 'and man's a fool!' . . . The peril and the labor, Prince, lie not in dreadful monsters or in mighty deeds, but in the keeping of the heart a man has won. This is the Dolorous Doom of one who rode not home to claim his lady's hand— that each and every Maytime till I die, I must be overthrown by love which once I overthrew."

Jorn was silent for a little space and then he said, "One

of your brothers, then, came back with golden tusks or a silver sword and won the lady's hand?"

The old man shivered inside his armor.

"She never wed, but sat with owls by day and cats by night, peering far and near and crying, 'Hark!' Her true love came in every form, in dust and wind and roses. Her

voice grew high and shrill and wild and wilder. And in the end she brewed an evil brew of mice and woad and coccatrice and rue, and over this she cast a spell in metaphor. The steel I wear is Strength, the flaw therein is Pride. Thunder how I will, I'm never safe inside." The old Knight blinked away a tear. "Men see her once in every Maytime, swinging like a smoky lantern in a tree. . . . Ride swiftly, Prince, and love ride with you."

The young Prince watched the aged Knight in silence and heard him out. "She named you Valiant," was all that

Jorn could say, "and placed the crevice in your armor not too near the heart."

There was a deep moaning from the armor as the figure of Duff of the Dolorous Doom clanked slowly away and was lost among the trees.

Prince Jorn hurriedly refilled the chalice with the scattered rubies and a moment later he was riding swiftly for the castle of his father, the silver chalice shining in his hand.

THE DARK ENCHANTMENT

Four knuckles rapped seven times on the door of the high room in the castle, and when the Princess bade her visitor to enter, King Clode strode in, and after him came Tocko and the Royal Recorder and the Royal Physician.

"We have three bitter things to say—a fact, a tale, and a conclusion," began Clode, and his heavy face turned red.

"If I may speak first, Sire," said the Princess, "I have a bitter doubt to say."

"Then speak your doubt," said Clode, "unless it touch the honor of my sons or me."

"Tut, tut, tut, tut," said Tocko, who was peering closely at the Princess.

"Tut me no tuts," said Clode. "I am in no mood this day for tutting."

He waved his hand and the Princess went on. "The doubt has come to me that since I cannot remember my name, perhaps I have no name to speak of. Perhaps I am a milkmaid or a kitchen wench."

"Tut, tut," said Tocko. "My mother was a country maid and often used to sing:

> *'When all the Princesses are gone,*
> *The country maids will still go on.'* "

"I have no contempt for any woman," said the Princess, "as long as she confesses who and what she is. And there are rules, decrees, and orders by which no maid of low estate or common blood may marry Jorn."

"Or Thag," said Clode.

"Or Gallow," said the Royal Recorder.

"My father used to sing a rhyme that went, in part," said Tocko:

> " *'Kings and Princes,*
> *Dolts and dunces—'* "

"You'll end your rhyme in the dungeon if you do not hold your peace!" cried King Clode. He walked over to the Princess, who was once more scanning the three roads with anxious eyes.

"I could swear, and almost do, in spite of facts I'm privy to, that you're a princess of the blood." He turned and addressed the others. "Mark the manner of her speech and the carriage of her head."

"And the slimness of her ankle and the smallness of her foot," said the Royal Recorder.

"And the highness of her forehead and the brightness of her eye," said Tocko.

"You are deceived by illusion," cried the Royal Physician, who had been quietly taking his own pulse but not counting it, for as a patient, he still considered himself sick, while as a physician he contended that he was well. "It's this confounded sorcery. I tell you nothing confuses the practice of medicine one half as much as sorcery. I recall a patient I had, a wizard, who could cause a tumor to dance all over his body and assume even the appearance of a flower or a jewel. Let us not be taken in by false shapes and semblances. What is, was— and what was, will be. I'll test the creature's heart."

"The *lady's* heart," said Clode.

"We'll go by seeming till we have the proof."

"I promised her a fact, a tale, and a conclusion," said Clode.

"I'll tell the tale," said Tocko.

"I'll draw the conclusion," said the Royal Physician.

"I'll state the fact," said the Royal Recorder. "It is a fact, then," he said to the Princess, "that you cannot remember your name."

"Tocko will tell the tale," said Clode.

"In point of fact," said the Royal Recorder, "and truth and count and number, there are more tales than one to tell. There's Tocko's tale, and nine besides, all identical, exact, and parallel."

"We'll stick to one," said Clode, "since they are all the same."

"I merely wish to state, avow, affirm, asseverate, maintain, confess, proclaim, protest, announce, vouchsafe, and say that there are precisely ten such tales in all, and each and every one duplicates, substantiates, corroborates, and proves each and every other."

"Don't wrap me up in words!" cried Clode. "Tocko, tell the tale!"

And Tocko told the tale of the white deer of a hundred years ago, and how it was in truth a deer and not a princess of the blood.

The Princess listened in silence, standing very still.

"The Royal Physician will draw the conclusion," ordered King Clode.

The Royal Physician, who had been saying "ah" to himself in a corner and tapping his chest and counting to nine, stepped forward.

"The conclusion to be drawn," he said, touching the tips of his fingers together, "the conclusion to be drawn is that you are in fact and in truth, beyond the shadow, question, or peradventure of a doubt—but stay, I did not test your heart." He placed his right ear against the breast of the Princess and listened, muttering "hm" and "ho" and "hm" again.

"The heart is much too high, *much* too high," he announced at last, "both as to location and rapidity of beat. There is a skip, a definite skip, such as might be brought on by too much leaping over brooks, *much* too much leaping over brooks, but I could not give a final opinion, of course, until I had examined the brooks."

The King scowled and looked away. "Draw the conclusion," he ordered.

"Ah, yes, the conclusion," said the Royal Physician. "The conclusion is that in all human probability—or should I say all *animal* probability?—but certainly not to all intents and *purposes*, you are, dear lady—dear creature, I should say —a deer. . . . Say 'ah,' " the Royal Physician added to himself, and he retired to a corner, saying "ah."

King Clode stared at the cold stone floor, his face still flushed; the Royal Recorder fumbled foolishly with a pocketful of seals and ribbons; Tocko's dim old eyes, no longer strong enough to see the moon or the stars, were soft with pity.

The Princess did not move except to lift her head a little higher.

"If you still cannot remember your name, then you *must*

be a deer," said the King.

"A princess would remember her name," said the Royal Recorder.

"Particularly in view of the fact that there is no evidence of a concussion severe enough to eradicate memory, and no marked dilation or contraction of the pupils of the eye to indicate the presence of a potion, philter, or other obliterant," said the Royal Physician. "Obliterant," he repeated, frowning. "*Is* there such a word?"

"You are perhaps thinking of 'eradicant,' " said the Royal Recorder. "Eradicant is a word, I believe, although when you repeat it, it *does* sound meaningless."

"Be done with this weighing of words, this measuring of meaning!" cried Clode. "Explain the nature of the spell, the rule of her enchantment."

The Royal Recorder cleared his throat and spoke.

"In enchantments of this kind—which I hold to be in extremely bad taste—the true deer, having assumed the face and form of a princess, finds it impossible, for obvious reasons, to retain the love of knight or prince or peasant, once her unhappy secret is revealed."

"Get on with it, get on with it," ordered the King.

" 'Love most certainly shall fail you thrice, thus runs the line and measure of your spell,' " intoned the Recorder solemnly. " 'When love has failed you thrice, you will resume the shape and semblance of a deer.' "

94

"And mind you, no more leaping over brooks. Bad for the heart," the Royal Physician said. "Mee, mee, mee, mee," he added, testing his throat for soreness.

"Alas and woe, unhappy doe!" the Royal Recorder cried.

"Hold your tongue, you saucy clerk!" said Clode. "This lady is a princess to the present sight, and shall be so addressed while still she stands on two legs, not on four."

The Princess spoke at last, her dark eyes clear and fearless. "I ask the right to tell my Prince, before he claims my heart and hand, this sorry tale," she said.

"Asked and granted, done and done!" Clode bowed. "And spoken like a princess."

The Royal Recorder cleared his throat again. "If it should chance, happen, occur, take place, or come to pass that this Prince or that or the other should still maintain his love for you, in spite of what has been, and truly is, and should be, why, then you will forever keep the shape and semblance of a princess. So reads the ancient spell, so runs the old enchantment."

Tocko stepped forward and raised his hand. "I beg you to remember, Clode, the mother of your sons once bore the shape and semblance of a deer, and yet she was in truth a princess of the royal blood."

"But damn it all, she knew her name!" cried Clode. "*This* pretty deer—"

"This *Princess,* by your own decree," the Royal Recorder said.

"This Princess, then—" Clode began again and flushed and turned away.

"I am what I will be," said the Princess. "I will be what I am."

"There's this to lift your heart," said Clode. "You were the swiftest deer that ever tried the strength and skill of men. No common oaf shall give you chase, as in the case of Tocko's father's deer. You're fit for kings and princes as you stand or as you run."

The room had clouded with darkness, and in the moment of silence that followed the King's high praise, there was a distant sound of many hoof beats. The King strode to the window and looked out.

"What magic's this?" he shouted. "Behold! Three trophies shine together! Three Princes ride as one! Their paths have crossed and joined where inch and second meet. There's miracle in this, and sorcery."

Tocko, the Royal Recorder, and the Royal Physician peered over King Clode's enormous shoulders and beheld Thag and Gallow and Jorn galloping for the castle gates, their trophies shining in their hands, their horses racing nose to nose as if in single harness.

The Princess, who stood with her back to the fading light of the window, her eyes closed, felt a hand take hers and heard the deep voice of Quondo the dwarf say, "Come." He led her from the room and down the winding stone stair and into the great circular chamber. He handed her into the high carved golden chair and squatted on the floor beside it at her right.

The circular room rang with the sound of running feet as the breathless King and his breathless retainers rushed in through one door, and the panting Princes rushed in through another.

Before the Princess in the golden chair could make the sorry tale of her enchantment heard above the stamping and the shouts, the Princes placed, all at the same moment, their trophies at her feet—Thag, the golden tusks of the great Blue Boar; Gallow, the Sacred Sword of Loralow, and Jorn, the silver chalice filled with rubies—the while they cried in perfect unison, "I claim your heart and hand!"

A heavy breathing silence fell at last and no man moved. The Princes knelt, each on one knee, their eyes upon the Princess. The King and his retainers stood like frozen men Quondo squatted, motionless.

The Princess rose, straight and fine and fearless, and spoke in her low and lovely voice, addressing the King: "I know not in what order to proceed. Three Princes kneel as one. Three trophies shine together."

The King scowled and turned to the Royal Recorder. "Announce the order," he commanded.

"This wonder is unknown, at least in my time," said the Royal Recorder.

"And in my time and in my father's," said old Tocko.

"But I should say, if you will so decree it—" said the Royal Recorder to the King.

"Decreed!" cried Clode. "Decreed, and done and done."

"Then let the eldest son speak first and so on, in that order."

"I cannot see a thing," said Tocko.

"Light the torches!" cried the King, and through the castle halls the order echoed: "LIGHT THE TORCHES! *Light the torches!* Light the torches!"

Twelve small men in yellow flashed about the chamber and in a moment flames flared from the circular wall. The Princess spoke, her sorrowful eyes on Thag.

"You claim the heart and hand of one who is in truth a

deer changed by whim of witch or wizard to the shape and semblance of a woman."

While the torches flared and flickered between the shields and lances on the wall, the Princess spoke again:

"By old remembered spells and ancient tales, by every mark and sign, three Princes claim the heart and hand of one who is in truth a deer. I know the perils you have known, the leagues forlorn, the weather borne, to lay your trophies at my nameless feet. Love me truly, fail me never— woman will I be forever; but if love shall fail me thrice, I shall vanish in a trice. So tells the tale, so runs the spell. Prince Thag, do you love me well?"

The eldest son of Clode rose to his feet. Without a word, he broke the golden tusks of the great Blue Boar in his hands and turned his back.

"Love has failed her once," moaned Tocko.

"Love me truly, fail me never, woman will I be forever; but if love shall fail me thrice, I shall vanish in a trice. So tells the tale, so runs the spell. Prince Gallow, do you love me well?"

Prince Gallow rose to his feet. Without a word he broke the Sacred Sword of Loralow across his knee, and walked away and turned his back.

"Love has failed her twice," whispered the Royal Recorder.

"Love me truly, fail me never, woman will I be forever; but if love shall fail me thrice, I shall vanish in a trice. So tells the tale, so runs the spell. Prince Jorn, do you love me well?"

"Love will fail her thrice," croaked the Royal Physician.

Prince Jorn rose to his feet and lifted the silver chalice filled with rubies.

"Throw wide the portals!" roared King Clode. "Let the white deer pass! Who reaches for his lance dies like a hog! Throw wide the portals, let the white deer pass!" And through the castle halls the order echoed: "THROW WIDE THE PORTALS! . . . *Throw wide the portals!* . . . Throw wide the portals! . . ."

The white figure that stood before the golden chair was still. All eyes were strained, all necks were craned as Prince Jorn raised the chalice.

"One could hear a petal fall," whispered the Royal Recorder.

"I cannot hear a thing," said Tocko.

"Silence!" roared the King. "And give her room! Denial's in Jorn's heart, all hear her doom!"

Prince Jorn spoke: "What you have been, you are not; and what you are, you will forever be. I place this trophy in the hands of love."

The Princess took the chalice in her hands

"You hold my heart," said Jorn.

As the young Prince spoke, the torches died to the tranquillity of candlelight, and April fragrance filled the room, and Jorn beheld a new and lovelier Princess than he had ever seen in life or dreams.

"The fragrance, if my memory serves," old Tocko said, "of lilacs."

"Sh-h," said the Royal Physician.

"Who is this Prince, this tall strange Prince who takes the chalice from the lady's hand?" whispered the Royal Recorder.

For out of nowhere in a tick of time a stranger had indeed appeared, a stranger tall and dark and young, who stood beside the lovely maid and held her chalice in his hands that she might descend the few steps from the golden chair and place her hand in Jorn's.

King Clode, who had seen the strange Prince at the same moment as the others, closed his eyes and rubbed them with his knuckles and opened them again. He took a step forward.

"Your name, your kingdom, and your cause!" bellowed Clode.

The tall Prince bowed to the King and spoke: "Before I name my name, my kingdom, and my cause, I seek a royal favor."

"Name its nature," said the King.

"A deed undone that long has wanted doing." The Prince set down the silver chalice on the golden chair.

The Royal Recorder cleared his throat. "The favor should be named, described, and specified," the Royal Recorder said. "It should be duly entered on a scroll and signed and sealed."

"Nonsense!" said the King. "I like the young man's eye. The favor's granted."

At this, the unknown Prince strode to where Thag and Gallow stood. He caught them up, one in each arm, and knocked their heads together seven times and set them down.

The King's loud laughter shook the iron shields on the wall. "What god is this who plays with men like puppets?" bellowed Clode.

The young Prince bowed.

"My name is Tel, your Majesty, and I'm the youngest son of Thorg, the mighty king of Northland."

"A rich and mighty monarch and, by all report, a good man in the saddle," said the King. He waved the young man on.

"You have my kingdom and my name, and now my

cause. Your Majesty, may I present, to you, your sons, and your retainers, my youngest sister, noble daughter of a noble King, affianced bride of brave Prince Jorn?" Prince Tel bowed deeply to the dark and lovely lady whose hand still clung to Jorn's. "Her Royal Highness, the Princess Rosanore of Northland."

Clode and his men were held as by a new enchantment, and for a long astonished moment, no one stirred and no one spoke. The face of Clode went all the colors of a flag before it found at last its normal flush of wine and weather.

"Lyres and fiddles!" bellowed Clode. "Meats and wines! What wine, on second thought, is fit for this occasion? Melt down a million rubies! But stay! On third thought, wine in bottles! The magic's turned my heart but not my stomach. Prince Tel and Princess Rosanore, I bid you warmth and welcome, health and joy."

"The case lacks precedent," the Royal Recorder wailed, "and, lacking precedent, is difficult, if not, indeed, impossible, to classify, co-ordinate, and catalogue. We have here terms of two distinct and unrelated sets of spells which overlap. Overlapping, in the legal sense, I heartily deplore." He babbled on, but no one listened.

There was a great running and scurrying and laughter and movement and a fine exchange of courtesy and compliment while lyres and fiddles played. The Royal Wizard produced a shower of silver stars, and a great table in the banquet hall was filled with meats and flowers and wine. Prince Tel sat at the head of the table beside the King, and on their right sat Rosanore and on their left sat Jorn. The King smote the table a heavy blow which set the crystal dancing.

"I knew her," said the King, "by the manner of her speech and the carriage of her head."

"I knew her," said the Royal Recorder, "by the smallness of her foot and the slimness of her ankle."

"I knew her," said Tocko, "by the highness of her forehead and the brightness of her eye."

"I knew her by the singing in my heart," said Jorn.

Thag and Gallow glowered at their plates.

"You are a dolt," said Thag.

"You are a dunce," said Gallow.

Clode stared about him into the dark places under the shields. "There is a stupid dwarf," he said to Tel, "who creeps about the night like cats."

"Like cats, or like a cat?"

"Like cats," said Clode. "He seems to sit in six or seven corners all at once."

"You've had him long?" asked Tel.

"Three months or so," said Clode. He drank off a tankard of wine. "Popped up one day, and I let him stay. A good hand with the horses and the hounds. And what is more, a better judge of men than I, in proof of which I owe the misbegotten clown a cask of gems. Never lost a wager with a lighter heart. I have a silly fondness for the dwarf. Can't say I ever showed it, though. I hope no harm's befallen him." Clode raised another tankard to his lips and drank and closed his eyes.

"Quondo's gone forever, Sire," said Tel in an old familiar rumble that the King remembered well.

The tankard clattered to the floor and Clode leaped to his feet and closed both eyes and opened one and stared at Tel.

"You're Quondo!" cried the King.

"I was," said Tel.

The King drank off another bowl of wine before he spoke again. "I like the taste of wine," he said, "the feel of leather. I'll ride or drink your father down in any weather. I am a hunter, sir, a fair man in the saddle. Ah, yes," his eyes shone, "in any weather. I have no mind for miracle, my friend, and were I king of all the kings, I'd make an end of magic. I have few graces, Tel, no doubt for lack of daughters, and if I have offended you, I humbly beg your pardon. Wizardry's a woefuler thing than wine, and it's befuddled stronger heads than mine." He drank deep from the bowl once more. "A deer's now Rosanore, a dwarf is Tel, what rhyme or signal broke the spell? Who could this dark enchantment bring upon the children of a king?"

He smote the table a great blow and called for silence.

"Magic bitter, magic sweet," Clode began. He groped for a rhyme and could not find it. "Has united the great house of Clode with the great house of Thorg." He drank from the huge bowl of wine. "A man I can outride and out-drink the best day he ever saw, though that's beside the present point. We have beheld a miracle this day which wants explaining. I give you young Prince Fel." He sat down and rose again with some effort. "Tel," he said, with great dignity, and resumed his chair.

All eyes were on the tall young Prince except the eyes of Thag and Gallow, who were muttering to each other.

"The wine has mulled your wits," said Thag.

"I tell you the Dragon has to be wound up," said Gallow, "with a great big key."

"Silence!" roared the King, and young Prince Tel rose to his feet and began the tale of his sister's enchantment and his own.

"My father, Sire, the great King Thorg of Northland, was loved by many damsels in his youth," the Prince began. "His feats in battle and the chase broke open the tender locks of half a hundred hearts."

"Powf!" said Clode. "Get on with it."

"One damsel was a dark and jealous wench named Na-grom Yaf, who, on the day my father wed the Princess of his choice, swore a frightful vengeance on his house.

"One year and twenty days ago the Princess Rosanore

and I were riding in the Wilderness of Gwain. The sun went down, the wind rose, and we were lost. A crooked moon came up and by its light we saw a creature lying in the grass, a creature like a vulture dead or dreaming. Before I could dismount, it seemed to rise and float before our eyes,

making horrid signs and symbols in the air. A witch, in the unspeakable employ of Nagrom Yaf, she cast her awful spells, the while we sat like stone on stony horses.

"Rosanore was changed into a deer which could be disenchanted only if and when a king and his three sons should bring the deer to bay, but even then she would not know and could not speak her name. But on such day and in such hour as she should hear a prince declare his love for her, in spite of doubt and dread and tattle-tale, the spell would break like crystal struck on stone, and she'd be Princess

Rosanore again."

King Clode was chewing his mustaches. "And what if young Prince Jorn here had not declared his love?" he asked.

"If love had failed my sister thrice," said Tel, "she would have wandered nameless all her life."

"These spells," the Royal Recorder said, "are shockingly untidy. These spells should all be written down and witnessed and attested. Of all assumptions in our law, the strongest one is this: *Scribendum est,* which is to say that if the scroll does not exist, the scroll does not exist. And if the scroll does not exist, the spell is null and void, violable, unviable, and fallible, and tolerable only to the gullible. These present spells, *i.e.,*—spells A and B, involving Rosanore and Tel, hereinafter to be referred to as One and Two, should either be recast or just ignored, as never having *been* in legal fact, which holds that if a thing that should not be, has been, it never was. It's vastly more elastic and rewarding than the mundane or ordinary fact, which holds that just because a thing has been, it was."

"Scribble, scrabble, scrubble!" said Clode.

"My own enchantment," Tel resumed, "was something else and other. I was changed into a dwarf possessed of all remembrance. I knew my name and Rosanore's, but lacked the power to name our names or tell our tale in language plain or roundabout to her or any other. But on such day

and in such hour as I should hear a prince declare his love
for Rosanore, in spite of doubt and dread and tattle-tale,
then I would be Prince Tel again. If love had failed the
Princess thrice, I would have been the squat dwarf Quondo
all my life."

"How came you here?" demanded Clode. "How came
your sister to our woeful woods?"

"She fled through twenty kingdoms in the year of our
despair," said Tel, "and always Quondo followed her a
hundred leagues behind. Minstrels, knights, and travelers
would point the way the swiftest deer in all the world had
gone, and I would wander on. I lost her in the snowy
months and wandered here, for men had told me tales of
your enchanted woods. Enchanted woods attract enchanted
things. My heart was high with hope. You were a king,

Sire, and your sons were three, as stipulated in the sorcery. I fed your hounds and horses for my keep and visited the magic woods each night, dropping softly from my chamber window to the ground. At last she came. I saw her flash like moonlight through the fireflies and the snow. I'd met a wizard in the woods, the mighty wizard Ro. I could not name my name to him, or Rosanore's, or tell our tale, but wizards have a way of knowing things. In guise of minstrel here one night, he sang you songs about a deer, a deer as swift as light—"

"I thought I knew the saucy varlet's face," roared Clode, "and said so at the time!'

The tall Prince smiled and went on with the tale.

"By this device and that device, the wizard played with time. I fancy Thag and Gallow were delayed, I fancy Jorn was speeded on his way. The wizard's magic brought the Princes riding home, not singly, but together."

"He must have been the round man in the tree," said Thag.

"He must have been the man in blue," said Gallow.

"He must have been the little man who told me why the cherries fall," said Jorn.

"I knew they rode by sorcery, and said so at the time!" cried Clode.

"I don't remember that you did," the Royal Recorder said.

"Nor I," said Tocko.

"Nor I," said the Royal Physician, who was striking his knee sharply under the table to test his reflexes.

"I do," said Rosanore. " 'There's magic here and sorcery!' he cried. I heard it clearly."

"As wise as she is lovely!" shouted Clode. "Surrounded by these dodderers and dolts, I blow my horn in waste land, so to speak." He picked up a fresh bowl of wine that had been set before him.

"So ends the tale of Rosanore's enchantment and my own," said Tel. "The rest you know." He bowed to the King and sat down.

"I blow my horn in waste land," repeated Clode, and since he seemed about to weep, the lyres and fiddles struck up a lively tune.

King Clode got to his feet and raised a tankard of wine. "Here's joy and jollity," he said to Rosanore and Tel and to Rosanore and Jorn. "And here's to Thorg, a mighty King, the second huntsman of his time. All drink!"

The lyres and fiddles played brightly and the Royal Wizard produced a flight of white doves and a shower of red roses.

The Royal Physician, who always sneezed when there were doves and roses, got up and backed out of the room, bowing and sneezing. In the darkness of the corridor out-

side the banquet hall he stumbled over a large and dreamy flop-eared dog and fell flat on his back. He limped up to his chamber, sneezing and protesting.

The Wizard produced a silver fountain and a golden rain above the lyres and fiddles.

Old Tocko rose to his feet and recited a legend for a sundial which had come to him as he watched Jorn dance with Rosanore, and Rosanore dance with Tel:

> *"As slow as time, as long as love:*
> *The rose, the fountain, and the dove."*

The Royal Recorder, who had drunk more wine than was his custom, recited laws of mortmain and chancery to himself.

King Clode rambled on above the music and the laughter. "Sing heigh and ho, and drink and dance, but not too long or late. Tomorrow when the sun is high we ride to Northland." He winced as he pronounced the name, and closed both eyes and opened one. "I still maintain I'd rather die than drink that northern wine. It's bleak as turtle tears and harsh as witches' spells. I swear the stuff is only good for rubbing rust from buckles and from bells." He raised a bowl of white Clodernium high above his head. "God bless us all!" he cried, and drank it off, and went to bed through the laughter and the music, the silver fountain and the golden rain, the roses and the doves.

The next day, when the sun would have marked the hour of noon on Tocko's sundials, if it could have got at

them, the King and his sons and Rosanore and Tel started off for Northland in full panoply and jingling trappings. A hundred mules brought up the rear, carrying two hundred casks of red and white and yellow wines.

EPILOGUE

There is a dusty yellow scroll written in the olden time, which tells that on the day and in the hour when Prince Jorn said to Roşanore, "You hold my heart," the dark and jealous Nagrom Yaf and the wicked witch in her employ were riven and shriveled by a bolt of lightning from the blue and removed completely from the world as by a strong and strange obliterant.

I find no cause to doubt the scroll, for it is signed and sealed, and witnessed, and attested.